SACRIFICIAL Waters

Copyright © 2024 by A.D Jones
All rights reserved.

No part of this book may be reproduced in any form or by any electronic or mechanical means, including information storage and retrieval systems, without written permission from the author, except for the use of brief quotations in a book review.

This book is a work of fiction. Any reference to real events, people, or places are used fictitiously. Other names, characters, places and incidents are the products of the author's imagination. Any resemblance to actual events, locales, or persons; living or dead, is entirely coincidental.

SACRIFICIAL
Waters

A. D. JONES

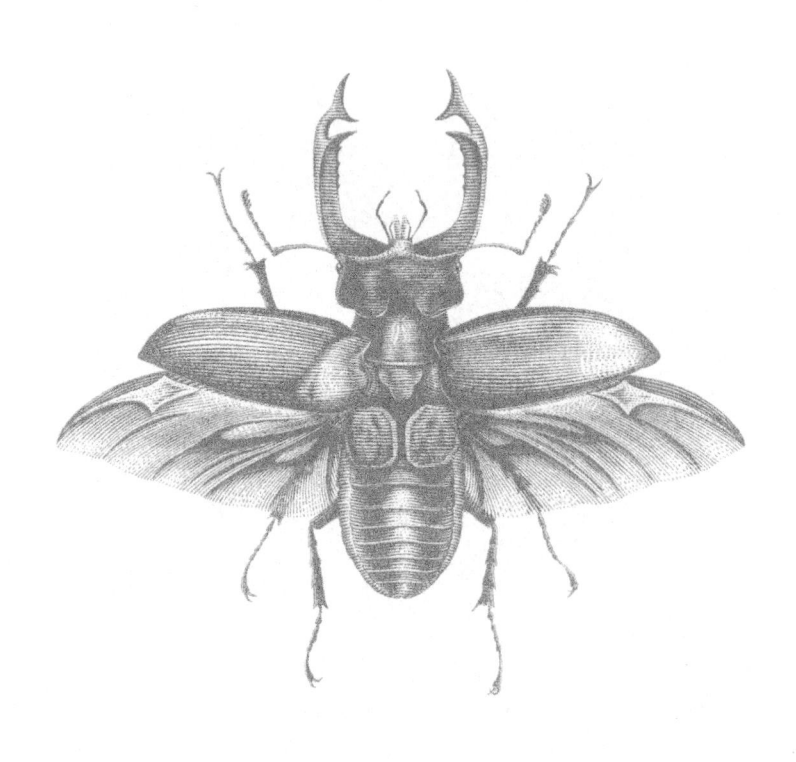

For my nephew Jacob,
Who's really excited to see the 'wit-thh'.

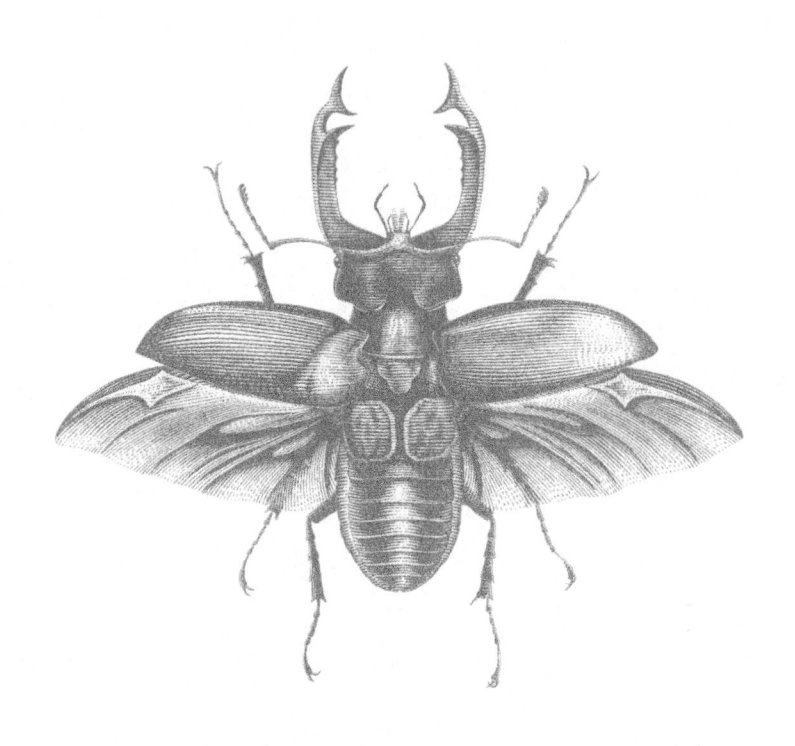

PROLOGUE

August 16th, 1993

The man with the gun stepped into the bank.

The pistol trembled in his shaky grip as he walked up the rough concrete steps between the gaudy stone pillars – pillars that were twelve hundred miles too far north of the Roman colosseums where they belonged. As he reached the end of the entrance vestibule, he released a defeated sigh and pushed open the glass doors with his free hand.

His greasy brown hair was plastered to his forehead, which in turn was slick with sweat. He wore a white Radiohead t-shirt depicting the album cover for Pablo Honey – a baby's face amid a sea of yellow centred the chest of this much stained shirt, the areas around both armpits discoloured and damp. More brown splotches were dotted about the shirt as well as two larger areas that were torn and circled with deep crimson blood stains. The filthy denim 501's he wore were caked in dried mud and at a rip in the knee another unhealthy amount of blood had soaked into the fabric.

His trainers too had the sepia tones of dried mud coating their entire surface.

Shivering, he limped into the air-conditioned building, his footsteps slapping against the smooth marble floor as he walked towards the centre of this spacious foyer.

Six people stood in line, waiting for their turn to step up and make their deposits or withdrawals. Two open counters were staffed by middle-aged women in navy blue uniforms, nestled safely behind reinforced glass barriers.

BANG.

The gunshot rang out as screams erupted from the crowd and they instinctively dove for cover, ducking down or scurrying behind counters, the ladies at the desks remaining motionless in their seats as both colour and composure drained from their faces.

The man stood frozen in the centre of the lobby; gun still pointed skyward as dustings of plaster fell upon him like dust motes dancing in the light before descending to earth. His eyes, though heavy and tired, locked on the woman behind the counter closest to him as he slowly arced the gun levelling it directly at her.

"This is a robbery," he announced as a grin crawled across his weary face. He prayed that movies hadn't mislead him too much and that at this moment, a silent button was being pressed under the desk, alerting the police to his presence.

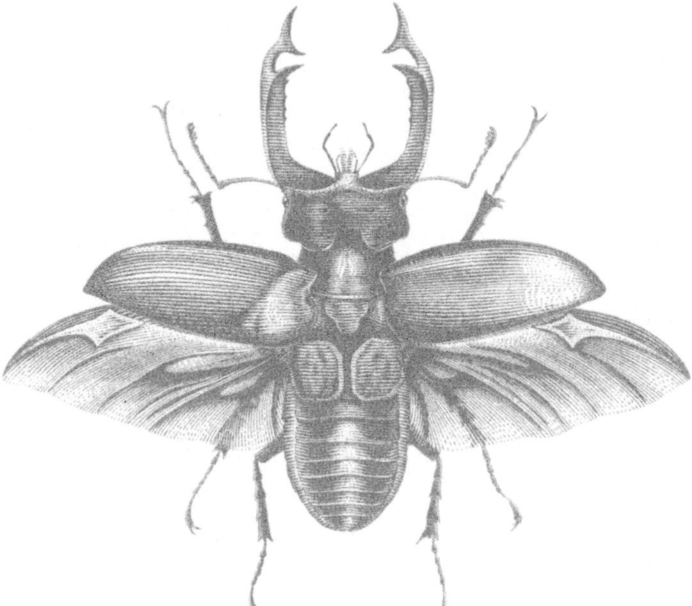

CHAPTER 1

July 19th, 2022

Rich sprang up from the sofa and ran to the kitchen with the grace of a toddler amid the droning beeps and thick black smoke that was assaulting his nostrils.

Grabbing the much-stained red oven glove that sat atop the hob, he pulled open the oven door, and the backdraft of heat hit him as the smoke began to billow out. Tears streamed from his eyes. He reached for the tray inside and pulled it out before dropping it onto the top of the oven, and the black charcoal disc that was once a frozen pizza lay there, almost artistic in its borderline incineration.

"Fucked it," he said as he wafted the air around it with the oven glove, his eyes still stinging.

Rich had learned a lot of things in the past few years, but cooking was sadly not one of them. His love for food wasn't something that could be disputed for sure, but the actual culinary arts had continued to defy him. Living off take-out was a much easier way to function, albeit a less healthy and more costly one.

The health aspect was something that he sometimes pondered late at night when he lay in bed staring at the ceiling and tried to remember when he had last eaten a vegetable. The cost element wasn't a factor to him at all. Rich could comfortably afford to buy takeaway food for the rest of his life.

He could in fact afford to buy most things.

People always say that winning the lottery will change your life – a statement he couldn't argue with. They don't, though, tell you that it could also ruin your life. The ability to do what you want can quickly transform into the freedom to do nothing, and while nothing is peaceful, it is also solitary and comes with its own downsides.

The irony of his name wasn't lost on him either. While yes, it was Richard on his birth certificate, he had gone by Rich since he was sixteen, and so becoming *Rich the millionaire* was both ironic and funny.

Three million, one hundred eleven thousand, three hundred forty-three pounds and sixty-four pence, to be precise. An insane amount of money to a twenty-nine-year-old admin assistant for Lloyd James Financial, a soul-destroying firm situated in a drab office building in the city centre, and a figure that easily justified giving the middle finger to the concept of working his two weeks' notice.

He had no real desire to travel the world or anything as extravagant as that. His desire was of a more anti-social nature. He wanted to do very little with his newfound free time. Read, play video games, binge watch movies and in general relax, all the while avoiding the tedium of the general public.

Perhaps he'd eventually get to sitting down and working on that novel he'd fantasised about writing; lord knows he had the time and the money to pass it around to the people who could polish it into a serviceable product.

Rich wasn't a stupid man. The fact that he wanted to withdraw from society, and that he'd gradually become nocturnal, coupled with the fact that he had slowly lost interest in the things he loved, were all glaringly obvious signposted symptoms of depression.

But he'd be damned before he resigned himself to laying on a chaise longue and talking it out with a balding nerd in a herringbone suit and a notepad.

He headed back into the front room and dropped onto the sofa.

After reaching for his phone on the coffee table, bypassing a mess of empty coke cans, crisp packets, and old chocolate wrappers, he began the tedious scrolling search for yet again another takeaway. It had just gone ten pm and so options thankfully were still varied.

The idea of pizza had been tarnished for now, and so he settled on a cheeseburger, milkshake, and a side of chicken wings, quickly finishing up his order before throwing the phone back down on the table and reaching for his laptop.

After booting it up, he did a cursory scan of the usual sites he frequented, social media being another of the things he found monotonous and dull – like returning to the fridge, you know there's nothing new there, but you keep looking anyway. Once he'd satisfied his curiosity by checking world events and that nobody he knew had died, he jumped across to the forums.

While his general distaste for people as a whole was strong, he liked to make the occasional outing into the world and had found urban exploring to be a perfect outlet for that. It was always sojourns into places people weren't supposed to be, and so apart from the occasional security guard or night watchman, who as a rule they were supposed to avoid anyway, it was just a handful of people who fell under the umbrella term of *weirdos* like himself and so were generally palatable in small doses.

Urb-Oboros was an Urbex forum set up by Francine Nightcrawler, *obviously not her real name*, and her partner, Dora. She was pleasant enough, though he continually felt the need to bite his tongue on the subject of her nom de plume; was she in fact aware that a nightcrawler was a worm, and not quite as cool a moniker as she perhaps thought.

The forum itself, though, was more like a meeting place for likeminded individuals in search of new places to explore, and Francine was always able to find new and exciting locations for them to visit, as well as the organisation of said trips. One such outing recently, to a large, abandoned home in Worcestershire where a man had seemingly perished in an unexplained caravan fire on the grounds, was quite the fun day out.

The forum's neon green text on black background loaded up, and he was met with the Urb-Oboros logo above the text 'Take nothing but pictures, leave nothing but footprints', which was the golden rule of urban exploring, though sadly one that many chose to ignore.

Already logged in, he clicked straight to the *upcoming events* section to check if there had been any changes in plans or times for tomorrow's trip.

Satisfied that things were unaltered; he closed the laptop and placed it back on the coffee table before him and settled in to wait for his food.

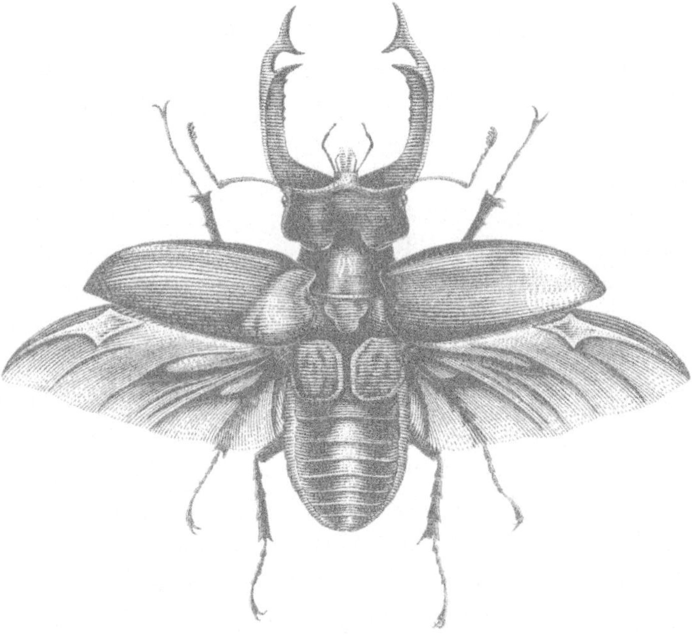

CHAPTER 2

"**D**id they catch whoever did it?"

Francine downed the last of the wine in her glass and placed it on the coffee table, knowing full well that there was still plenty more in the bottle next to it.

"Hmm? Oh, I have no idea," she said as she took in Dora's expression of twisted excitement. "I didn't really think to ask. I just know it's been abandoned since it happened, and that was nearly thirty years ago."

She watched Dora fidget on the sofa, sat with her legs crossed as she always did. It didn't look particularly comfortable, but who was she to tell somehow how to sit?

"But a bunch of people were killed?" she asked still excited by the prospect of their trip.

This was Dora's murder podcast, delivered to her in real time.

"Yeah, a total bloodbath apparently. Whole group of them, all killed in some gruesome fashion." She paused for a second before giving Dora a crooked grin. "You're a proper ghoul, you know that right?"

"Hey, you're the one dishing out the gory details. Did you expect me not to get a little bit excited? Besides you know you love me for it anyway."

Francine watched as Dora stuck out her lower lip and gave her the cute, puppy dog eyes. "Yeah, okay. Maybe."

She picked up the wine bottle and began to refill her glass as Dora necked the rest of hers like a vodka shot and placed her glass down on the table, nudging it closer as she wiggled her eyebrows at her.

Francine topped up both glasses and lifted hers to take a sip. It might have seemed odd to celebrate a new exploration before it happened, but a new adventure was always exciting for her, and she couldn't help feeling giddy. The pair didn't need much of an excuse to celebrate anyway.

"I am glad you're able to make this one though, I've got a good feeling about it."

"I bet. Abandoned youth hostel that served as the final resting place for a bunch of people, I'm sure Sophie is literally creaming her jeans at the thought," Dora said, sipping delicately at her fresh glass.

Francine chuckled to herself. "Yeah, something like that. Grace is pretty fired up for it too. You'd swear that

I told the pair of them that there were guaranteed ghosts at this one."

"Don't ruin the illusion. I'm hoping for that myself."

"Stranger things have happened." Francine shrugged. "What about the boys?"

Francine thought about the men that made up their little group, each of them very much a different person, but all of a similar mindset.

"You know what guys are like," she said. "They're reluctant to buy into anything that they can't rationalise. They love a good poke around places they're not supposed to be though, so I'm sure they'll be happy regardless. No apparitions required."

A silent moment of contentment passed and, as if on cue, the niggling doubt reared its head and begin to eat away at her.

The safety of the group was of utmost importance to her, but she also needed to guarantee an enjoyable excursion too. After her love for Dora, Urb-Oboros was the most important thing in her life, and she was fully aware that a boring trip could be the death of things and that the collective she had worked so hard to build could fall apart as easily as a house of cards.

Her efforts crashing down to nothing.

Click.

"Oi." Dora snapped her fingers in front of her face. "Get out of your head. I can see what you're doing."

Francine quickly shook herself free of the feelings of doubt. "Sorry. You're right. It's going to be good."

"That or we'll all get murdered by some maniac. Either way, it'll be exciting."

She rolled her eyes. "I fucking love you, you know."
"So you should," Dora smiled. "I'm a delight."

CHAPTER 3

Sophie knelt on the floor of the bedroom, her heels digging into her bum as she poised in front of the tall mirror, liquid eyeliner in hand. She steadied herself for the third attempt at getting the wing of her eye make-up to match her right eye. Her focus deepened as her tongue protruded past her lips, as if she were removing the wishbone piece in the game of Operation, though there would be no buzz or glowing nose to signify her failure here – just a smudged eyelid.

"Jesus Christ, this is infuriating," she said as she hovered the ink clad tip of the pen inches from her eye.

"Cousins, not sisters. Remember," said her boyfriend Aaron from the comfort of the bed, where he was currently sprawled out on the much creased, black silk sheets, phone inches from his face as he scrolled listlessly through Instagram.

"That's eyebrows, dickhead."

"Oh. Well please tell me you've already done those or we're gonna be here all night."

A post-box-red stiletto landed on the bed with a thud, missing him by mere inches and bouncing before it came to a stop next to his face.

"It's alright for you, you don't have to spend forever putting your face on," she said with an air of frustration as she returned to the task at hand.

"Neither do you." He gave up on his phone, dropping it to his side as he sat up. "We're going to wander around an old, abandoned hostel or whatever this place is. I don't think the group of miscreants we're spending the time with are going to give a shit what you look like. Unless you're making an effort to look good for Chris?"

"Bleurgh." She forced her tongue out in a mock gag. "I don't think Chris is there for the ladies, do you?"

"No, I suppose not. I think he's just on the search for his mothership, to be honest." Having lasted all of thirty seconds without it, his iPhone was now back in hand and the doomscrolling commenced.

Bearing witness to their conversation were over sixty, twelve-inch tall, plastic dolls displayed on the two tall black bookshelves on the far wall, that were shaped like coffins. Each doll was an amalgamation of creepy and cute. Sinister Barbie dolls in various levels of gothic or satanic make-up and clothing, and in some instances various states of mortality – undead yet adorable toys with flowing synthetic hair and giant cartoon eyes, watching from their vantage point on the shelves.

Deciding she was happy with the fourth round of eyeliner, she dug around in the small black case that was open in front of her, her fingers acting like a digger as she ploughed through lipsticks, mascara, and a wealth of cosmetic paraphernalia until she came up with a candy red lip-gloss. Her mouth assumed the shocked expression of a cheap blow-up doll as she smoothed the glittery liquid across her lips. "I just assume he doesn't really have a lot of friends, but he's harmless enough, I suppose."

Aaron jumped off the bed and headed over to the desk to plug his phone in to charge. "Probably, but urban exploring is a bit of a weird niche to throw himself into. I guess chess club was fully booked."

"Maybe he's scoping out places to hide bodies in the future," she said as she started to throw things back into her make-up case. She still wasn't completely satisfied with the end result, but she knew once Aaron started pacing it was his subtle reminder that she was cutting it short for time. They'd been dating for four years, living together for over three, and she had learned to read him like a book. She had all his ways of silently conveying his thoughts down to a fine art.

She gave herself a final once over in the mirror, adjusting her crooked septum piercing before tousling her wavy, chestnut brown hair with her fingers and popping her lips like a great catfish as she checked her lip-gloss. "Do we know who else is going tonight?"

"Francine is bringing Dora along," Aaron said, his eyes staring vacantly into space as he engaged his breakdown of the assembly. "Chris is coming, of course and Rich, Grace, Victor, and I think Jack as well. Pretty solid turn out it, would seem."

"Yeah, not bad. I'm going to head down and feed the cats and then I think we're good to head off."

THE DRIVE TO THE MEETING PLACE FRANCINE HAD SET UP took about forty minutes and Sophie spent most of that time daydreaming and watching the streetlights slowly come alive as they whizzed past, the background noise of the radio's 80's playlist blaring out such classics as Poison by Alice Cooper and Here I go again by Whitesnake.

Sophie was more excited than usual about this coming trip, the nervous energy inside her starting to bubble to the surface. While she did really enjoy the whole Urbex scene in general, her true desire was to eventually find herself in the presence of the supernatural. Ghosts were something she'd been fascinated by since she was a child, and the very possibility of a sighting was something she truly longed for.

Tonight's exploration was to take place in an old youth hostel that Francine had discovered, and both the setting and nature of its violently deceased inhabitants, made her hopeful that this might be the trip she'd been waiting for.

CHAPTER 4

Francine sat on the bonnet of her Astra, phone in hand and checking the forum for any last-minute cancellations when the blue Ford Kuga pulled into the car park.

The Ford pulled into an open space and Francine watched as Sophie exited the passenger side, her black and white striped tights signalling her arrival as she waved from across the gravel before heading in Francine's direction.

Aaron then stepped out of the car in black jeans and a t-shirt complete with an indecipherable band logo and smoothed his dark hair back across his head before surveying the area. "Evening folks," he shouted into the far corner where the early arrivals had gathered.

Dora and Rich were standing by Rich's boxy grey Jeep, chatting with Grace, and Francine could barely peel her eyes away from Rich's sickly pale flesh, which practically glowed in the dim light, making Grace's deep brown skin look almost ebony in contrast. Across from them, Victor was still sat on his moped, looking helpless as Chris rambled into his ear.

"Victor!" Aaron called out. "Come and check this out a sec!"

Victor stepped off his moped, patted Chris on the shoulder and gave him a nod before walking over to Aaron.

Sophie reached Francine as she hopped down from the bonnet of the car and came forward to embrace her in a firm hug.

"As always, glad you could both make it," Francine said as she relaxed her grip. "Decent numbers tonight, it should be a good one."

"Yeah, Aaron mentioned. I'm looking forward to it." Sophie beamed as she messed with her hair.

Francine caught Dora's attention and seeing that Chris had joined her and Rich, beckoned them over with an upwards nod of her head. "We're just waiting on Jack and then we can head in, I think."

"Well, like I said, I'm excited. Is it far?" Sophie asked.

"Not really. About a fifteen-minute walk from here, shouldn't be too bad."

Aaron and Victor headed over to the group at the same time as the others, Aaron giving Rich a playful pat on the back before waving to the rest of the gathered party.

"Didn't feel like dressing discreetly then?" Aaron said as he nodded at Grace's bright red tank top.

"Dick," Grace said, laughing as she punched him in the shoulder. "I didn't think this was to be an overly stealthy one."

"Don't worry, you're fine," Francine interjected. "As far my research shows, there's no security or anything with this one."

Everyone milled about making their greetings and pleasantries before moving onto their expectations for the coming exploration. Sophie sounded excited to hear that Dora was also on a ghost hunt, which made sense to Francine as she didn't often tag along with their excursions.

Chris soon pissed on their bonfire as he began to reel off all the reasons why ghosts weren't real, but the rest of the group had learned, just like with a child, to let him carry on until he tired himself out.

The daylight had long since disappeared and here in this small carpark circled by trees, the darkness shrouded them like a personal eclipse.

It was just after ten, but for a mid-July night it was still warm enough to be comfortable, everyone dressed for the summer weather apart from Chris who for some unknown reason seemed to live in his blue and red Berghaus waterproof.

The blinding white headlights of Jack's Audi illuminated the crowd as he turned into the car park, casting their shadows thirty feet high behind them like creeping demons and causing everyone to shield their eyes from the glare.

After parking up and killing the lights, Jack stepped out of the car and waved to the gathered collective. Even with the darkness back in its rightful place, Jack's towering stature was clear. A little over six feet tall, with an athletic physique to go with it, jack cut quite the shadow in his denim jeans and white, form-fitting under armour sports shirt.

"Am I late?" he asked as he walked towards the group.

"Yeah, the testosterone convention was last week," Aaron joked.

Sophie elbowed him in the ribs and gave him a stern look.

"You're good, we all got here early is all." Rich stepped forward to shake his hand.

"Good to see you, Jack," Francine said. "I don't think you've met Dora. Dora – Jack. Jack – Dora." She said as she levelled a finger gun at each of them and swung it back and forth.

"A pleasure." He leaned down to hug her, enveloping Dora's petite frame.

"We have spoken on the forum, I think," Dora said as they broke away.

Francine spun on the spot and gave each of them a quick cursory glance. An overweight, pallid Rich contrasting with the statuesque physique of Jack; a balding middle-aged man in a raincoat; an eastern European on a moped; Grace, at just twenty-four, the baby of the group; and two couples, one straight and one gay. "Okay, great. Well, that's everyone. Let's get going. Follow me."

They walked for fifteen minutes, weaving through the tall trees, the cool summer breeze a welcome sensation on their skin as they followed a faint trail on the ground left by years of repetitious footfall, until their destination became visible in the distance.

The once grand Edwardian building was set back from the trees, its combination of red and white brickwork now coated in moss, vines, and other plant life. The dark slate roof ran the width of the house with three smaller gabled roofs jutting out from its side. These too had seen much better days, and tiles were missing from multiple areas across the slate.

Francine brought a hand up into the air as she stopped, halting their journey. "Okay, guys, we all know the rules. From here on out tread extremely carefully, look out for broken glass and heaven forbid, needles. Don't wander too far on your own and with stairs and upper floors, if you're not sure it's gonna take your weight, just don't."

"Why did you look at me when you said that?" came Rich's voice.

Francine let out a massive sigh. "I'm not even looking at any of you, shut the fuck up, Rich."

As they began making their way towards the front of the house, Aaron nudged Chris with his elbow. "Do you think my emotional baggage counts?"

Chris, who'd been fiddling with the Nikon camera around his neck, stopped and stumbled over his words trying to find a response as Grace shoved Aaron forward. "If it did, you're probably best just waiting out here. I'll take real good care of Sophie for you." She smirked.

He brought both palms up in a gesture of surrender. "Very funny. I was also going to ask if she thought the size of my balls would be an issue."

"Aaron!" Sophie snapped. "Stop."

Up ahead, Francine took point with Dora, stepping into the open doorway, the door itself horizontal, hanging from the lower hinge. She ushered everyone into the building one by one and followed behind with Dora taking up the rear.

They found themselves in a narrow corridor that opened into a larger hallway. A set of stairs led to the upper floor and doorways were set on each side of them, one to the left and two to the right, with a final doorway straight ahead past the stairs. The once white wallpaper was yellowed and peeling and the whole hallway smelled damp and mouldy.

The building was heavy with an ominous sense of dread, and Francine felt the goosebumps on her arms as they made themselves known. Lifting her foot, she peeled a weathered sheet of paper from the sole of her shoe and was about to cast it back to the ground when something on it caught her eye.

It was a portion of a map, that looked to be around the area of the Peak District. A large cross was etched into a part of the forest in red pen.

Interesting.

She thought she knew someone who would be able to take a look into it for her, and decided to fold and pocket the sheet of paper.

"Right, there's nine of us here, so if you're splitting up, stay in pairs at least," Francine said.

"Maybe we should stick together for now?" Chris suggested as he glanced into the room on his right, which looked to have once served as a waiting area.

"Shut up, nerd," Aaron countered. "We're going upstairs, who's coming?"

After a brief period of discussion, Aaron, Sophie, Rich, Grace, and Victor decided to carefully head up the wooden staircase to the first floor and left the others to look around the ground level.

The upper level was a long narrow corridor with wooden flooring and a threadbare runner carpet stretching along the middle of the ground. Six doors, three a side led from the hallway on the left, with four more, again two each side leading to the right.

"Time to split up again," Rich said. "Girls to the right, guys to the left and meet in the middle?"

"Like a school disco," Aaron joked.

Grace shrugged nonchalantly. "Fine with me. You boys scream if you see anything, and we'll come save you."

"Wonderful," Rich said as he began to tread carefully down the hall.

Aaron and Victor followed behind him and they soon found themselves outside a white wooden door, the many layers of paint, chipped and bubbled in places. Although the number appeared to have been removed, the faded paint beneath confirmed they were at room one. Rich grabbed hold of the brass doorknob and slowly turned it with a creak and began to push open the door.

Stepping inside, they were met with very little. Another stained and threadbare carpet, an old bedframe turned on its side and a small chest of drawers with each drawer removed and piled together in front of it. The glass in the window was smashed and coated the floor inside the room.

They moved back out into the hallway and repeated the process for two more rooms, finding much of the same in there.

"Not very exciting," Victor said as they closed the door on room three.

"Sometimes nothing is better than the alternative," Rich said. "Let's keep looking."

He thought about the things that they had found on previous outings, and if he was being honest with himself, it was never particularly eventful. Graffiti, used needles and if they were really lucky, like that weird old cottage, some satanic looking shrines set up with animal bones and long dead candles.

The fourth room was once again a repeat of the previous three, and Rich was beginning to think they should just head downstairs and see how the others were faring when he heard a high nasal moaning coming from behind him.

His mouth went dry, and after a second of panic, he spun on his heels and locked eyes on Aaron, the source of the noise. Aaron's face was a strange rictus of pain as he emitted this moaning, humming hybrid, before stopping and grinning at him.

"If there's nothing exciting, we might as well make it fun for the girls," he said before continuing.

"Child," Rich scolded as he moved back out into the corridor, Victor following behind like a lost puppy.

The girls had finished their inspection of the four rooms on their side and were stepping back into the corridor at the same time, looking across at Rich and Victor.

"Anything?" Sophie asked.

Aaron's moaning could still be heard from inside the room, but nobody appeared to be fooled by his attempts.

"Nope, just bedrooms, but we've still got these two, I guess," Rich said.

Sophie and Grace moved across the staircase to join the others as Aaron, still moaning, appeared back in the corridor. After a filthy look from Sophie shut him up, he leaned in to kiss her on the forehead as they all turned towards room five.

Rich took the brass handle once again and flung the door open. They were met with another facsimile of the previous rooms, only this time at the far wall under the window there was a cot, painted white with its wooden slats still seemingly pristine. They all crowded the doorway and peered at what appeared to be a wrapped bundle laying in the centre of the cot's mattress.

"No, thank you," said Grace, breaking the silence.

"It's fine," Rich said unconvincingly. "Just a blanket, that's all."

They moved in unison, taking baby steps into the room as they approached the cot, Rich in the lead as they crept forward. The very air felt like it had been squeezed out of the room, and the silence was deafening as they drew nearer.

Reaching the cot, Rich leaned over and slowly reached out to touch the wrapped bundle before him, his fingers inches from the blanket.

"Everything good here?"

They all leapt as one as Sophie screamed.

"Jesus Christ. You creepy fucking bastard," Aaron screamed at Chris, who was standing in the doorway with Jack beside him.

A white blur flew past them and hit Chris in the chest as he fumbled to catch it. Chris frowned at Rich, the sender of the projectile—the blanketed bundle from the cot—and unwrapped the blanket with trembling hands to reveal the rigid, plastic, baby doll it concealed.

"Are you finished giving us all a heart attack?" Rich said as he leaned back on the now empty cot.

Jack's face was a picture of sheer joy, and a massive smile spread across his lips as he took in the array of shocked faces. "We just thought we'd come see how you were getting on," he said. "It's pretty uneventful downstairs."

"Oh, it's going great. If you can smell piss, that was here already."

"Right, so as thrilling up here then. Gotcha."

AFTER MEETING UP DOWNSTAIRS AND TAKING IN THE REST OF the building, half the group still slightly shaken up, they decided to call it quits and made their way back to their vehicles in the carpark.

Making it back in good time, they began the ritual of saying their goodbyes until the next time. Francine was more disappointed than most with their trip and Dora was busy trying her best to console her.

"It's honestly fine," Grace said. "They can't all be exciting."

"Yeah, you've gotta sift through the dirt to find the gold, right?" Jack joined in.

She was still crushed by the lack of excitement but took their commiserations well. Her fingers grazed the piece of the map in her pocket, and she made a mental note to get this location looked into as soon as they got home. "The next one," she said as she kicked a small rock across the ground and into the trees. "The next one will be different. I promise you."

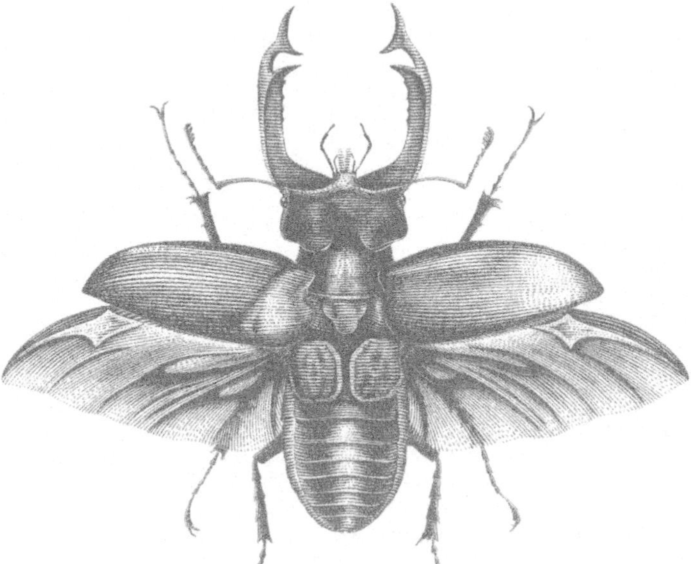

CHAPTER 5

The glorious summer evening slowly shifted as the grey storm clouds began to gather in the sky, darkening the horizon for many miles as they opened into a hammering downpour of rain. A deluge of biblical proportions covered the whole north of England, battering down on cars and rooftops alike, the din apocalyptic and constant.

Across the city, people stepped out of their homes and into their gardens, arms raised to the heavens, as they let the torrential rain wash over them in a refreshing baptism from the sky. A well needed break from the sticky heat of summer.

A balding, middle-aged man squatted over a tray of liquid, and its foul chemical stench permeated the entirety of the darkroom in his garage. He pinned photographs to the strips of wire that ran the length of the room, completely oblivious to the rhythmic pitter-patter of rain falling on the roof above him. He paused mid task to take another look at the slimy photograph in his hands – a dilapidated waiting room in a derelict youth hostel from a recent trip.

Inside a small two-bedroom house situated at the end of a quiet street, a couple lay on their bed listening to the rain beat down outside their window as they discussed bigger and better ideas for locations to visit with their little online community. Both women found themselves taking turns to play the optimist, while the other worried about the future of their endeavours.

Elsewhere in town, a tall man in a sweat soaked t-shirt, joggers and pristine white trainers stepped out of the gym and into the flood of rain as he made his way across the carpark to his black Audi A3, stopping at the door to let the cool water wash over him for a moment before lowering himself into the driver's seat.

On the second floor of an impressive, detached house tucked away in a small cul-de-sac, a millionaire tossed and turned in bed, as the skies emptied around him.

Much further away in a solitary prison cell, devoid of all but a single bed, a muscular man in his fifties, heavily scarred, his head closely shaven, screamed his throat raw as inmates from the surrounding cells shouted abuse and obscenities in his direction.

Further still, nestled deep in the forest, the rain whipped through the densely packed trees, beating down through the tall leafy branches before being carried by the wind into a horizontal shower crashing hard into the entrance of a small cave hidden away in the side of an enormous sandstone mountain; the opening a mass of compacted stone and rubble, with a hole just large enough for a grown man to squeeze through.

Shrouded in darkness, legs crossed beneath her, sat a woman. Her hair was lank and dark and hung over her face like tar dripping down her skull. Naked but for an ageing loincloth of tan animal hide covering her crotch, her skin was brown and leathery, the texture of tree bark, and her emaciated form was withered, her ribcage protruding and skeletal. The deflated shape of her breasts sagged and rested on her potbellied stomach, the rough, almost black nipples, circled by weeping sores.

She watched, through sunken hollow eyes as the rain dripped through a hole in the ceiling above her, splashing down and rippling across the water below. Her bared teeth were crooked and yellow, with grooved brown ridges of decay running through them, like brittle beetle wings.

A blackened tongue ran across thin cracked lips, leaving a trail of yellow, viscous, saliva in its wake before the lips slowly drew back into an unsettling rictus grin as she heard the movement from a tunnel far off in the distance.

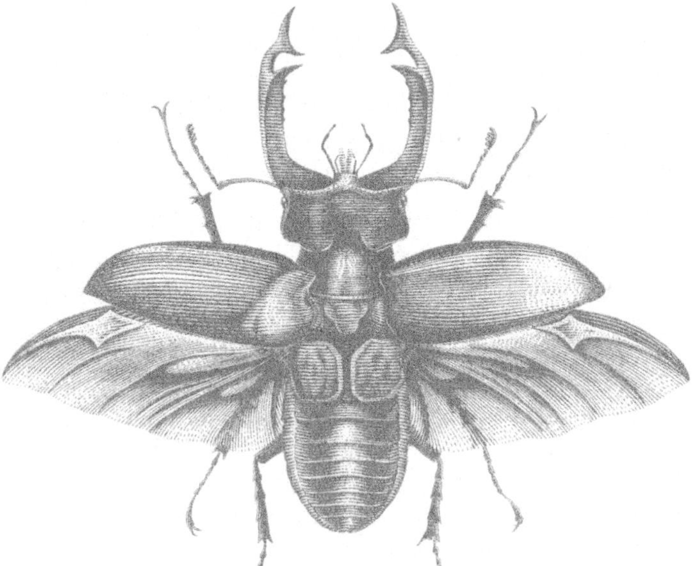

CHAPTER 6

"**W**hat if it's just running out of steam?"

Francine's crossed legs took up the whole corner of the L bend sofa in her front room, as she snuggled beneath her purple, oversized hoodie blanket, which was adorned with colourful cartoon narwhals. It swamped her, leaving her looking like a giant, deflated marshmallow.

Dora looked up at her as she paused rolling the joint in her hands, her reassuring smile from the other side of the room enough to ease Francine's immediate tension. The group was important to her, but Dora was truly her anchor in even the worst storm.

After what she'd consider a fairly textbook childhood, Francine had struggled once she moved into higher education. The separation of high school friends when they all branched off in different paths with their academic lives meant making friends again in college. A task she would come to find infinitely harder. *Do you like climbing trees? Me too!* Wasn't going to cut it with the disenfranchised teenage populace of Runshaw college, where she'd settled on taking A-levels in film studies, English literature, and politics.

She had come to realise that she was a pretty awkward teen and reaching the point in life where social interaction wasn't forced via the medium of classmate birthday parties, complete with jelly, birthday clowns and party bags – being left to friend making off her own inherent merits as a human was a positively herculean task. Adding the burgeoning realisation of her sexual preference towards same sex into the mix only added to this hormonal hell.

Accepting the proffered joint that Dora passed her from the other side of the sofa, she took a long drag and held it in her lungs a while before slowly exhaling and passing it back.

"I don't think it's going to run out of steam," Dora said as she accepted the joint back and took a pull. "There really are only so many places that you can get into to explore, it's going to take time to find them." She let the smoke slowly escape through her nose, the gentle burning on the exhale, a comforting feeling. "And some of them are bound to be better than others."

Francine had gotten through the two years of college with a good academic score, but a not so good accumulation of new friends. She had tried to integrate a little and she wasn't exactly ostracised, but nothing really stuck beyond being part of bigger group outings. Most of these were so alcohol fuelled that if the topic wasn't *who's round is it?* Or *shall we get shots?* it didn't exactly amount to much.

During this time, she did have the chance to finally engage in her first kiss, as well as the second, third and fourth, but she had also found that if you put enough alcohol into a teenage girl's belly and shake it around on the dance floor, they mostly became temporary bisexuals; so it really didn't amount to much.

Francine made it to her early twenties before she found herself in an actual relationship. Being what people referred to as a 'lipstick lesbian', or a lesbian that maintained the traditional feminine things ascribed to women – girly clothing, make-up etc, it made finding a partner that little bit more difficult as your sexuality wasn't the glowing, halo beacon that you wanted it to be. Discovering gay bars in the city had opened doors that made things a little easier and she managed to notch up a few encounters that would cement her sexuality even further, but it still took a few awkward nights and even more awkward mornings before she met Tink, who would be her first actual girlfriend.

"Yeah, I'm sure you're right." Francine picked at her nails, the rhythmic clicking an annoying background noise. "I just feel like that last one was a complete shitshow and I don't want to follow it up with another disappointment."

Dora tucked her long blonde hair behind her right ear, the last few inches of it a bright candyfloss pink and let out a sympathetic sigh. "I get that. I really do, but you must realise that everyone turns up because they want to. They don't have to. Also yeah, it's different, but this next one sounds like it could be really cool, so maybe stop being such a girl and relax a little, okay?"

"Woman's prerogative," Francine said with a wink as she relaxed a little.

Dora grabbed at her chest, gripping both breasts through her oversized white t-shirt with the vigour of a horny teenage boy and jiggled them up and down in tandem without breaking eye contact with Francine. "Feels like I'm one of those as well. Uno reverse," she said with a giggle. "Stop getting your knickers in a twist."

"Was that just for confirmation?" she asked. "Or can anyone have a go at that?"

"I suppose if you're going to stop moping, I can allow you to come over here and check my credentials," she said as she leaned back across her half of the sofa to make room.

Francine pulled the hoodie up over her head, leaving just grey joggers and a black vest top, her many tattoos now on display, the large, winged skull in the centre of her chest peeking out over the top of her clothes. "Okay, you're right, this cave does sound promising I guess," she said as she seductively made her way across the sofa like a cat.

"That's my girl. You tell me about this cave and maybe I'll let you explore mine," Dora said, sticking out her tongue.

Francine continued to move forward, starting to kiss up Dora's bare legs. "You're disgusting."

"And that," she paused. "Is why you love me."

CHAPTER 7

Jack pushed the key into the slot of the steel locker in front of him, wiggling it as it resisted, before it finally opened with a metallic clatter.

The sweat-soaked vest clung to his body as he reached into the container for his backpack. Stepping back, he dropped down on the wooden bench behind him and began to dig a fresh t-shirt out of his bag, the comforting ache of his muscles a reminder of the previous two hours.

The fluorescent lighting in the gym's changing room was as ethereal as always, and though the lingering smell of sweat was present, the dominant scent in the air was the chlorine filled pool wafting through a far set of doors.

A smell that reminded jack of his childhood. The nostril burning chemical stink, the pink stinging eyes, the sounds of flip-flops and wet feet slapping on tiled floors.

Pure nostalgia.

Sitting around a cheap plastic table with vending machine crisps, snacks, and a twenty pence plastic cup of powdery hot chocolate. The white noise of other people, and the humid closeness of the very air around him.

He took a moment to glance around the locker room, taking great lengths to avoid eye-contact with the older guys who'd long since given up on the idea of shame as they stood towelling their pasty, wrinkled naked bodies. He wondered if there was a point in their lives when they just woke up one morning and decided it was time to start a gym routine. Was there a day they caught sight of their naked, flabby forms in the mirror and knew it was time to do something about it, or was this part of some doctor prescribed health regime?

For him it was an entirely health-based focus. At thirty-three years of age, and as someone who visited the gym on four out of the seven days in a week, he had a decent amount of muscle mass and tone to show for it, but that wasn't his goal. He didn't come to the gym to bulk up, not that there was anything wrong with that, he was here to maintain a healthy body.

Having both a diabetic mother and a father with high blood pressure, it was easy to see the downfalls of an unhealthy life, and this was something that scared him more than he cared to admit.

Pulling the vest over his head, he began to towel over the damper patches of his body before throwing on his fresh t-shirt. He didn't like to shower at the gym, and this would do until he got home. He began to transfer his keys and wallet to his pockets and then picked up his phone.

One new notification.

'Urb-Oboros: one new topic.'

THE CHAIR CREAKED AS CHRIS LOWERED HIMSELF DOWN into the glossy brown leather recliner that sat facing the TV in his living room before moving the tray of food onto his lap.

Yellowfin tuna steak with a side of seared asparagus and a simple salad. There was something satisfying about preparing food like this, and while he was no Gordon Ramsay, taking simple ingredients, lemon juice, olive oil, garlic and thyme and mixing it all up to coat the steak before adding a liberal amount of salt and pepper, was oddly fulfilling.

It was no masterpiece, but he thought it would serve him well if he was to have a guest of the female persuasion over for dinner.

Not that the odds were very high on that front.

He settled himself in the chair and picked up the remote to find something on Netflix that could serve as a background visual to his meal. Eating in silence held a real sense of sadness that he didn't really want to let in.

The minimalist aesthetic to the room would be apparent to anyone stepping in. A single three-seat recliner rested against the wall, facing the entertainment centre, complete with 65-inch TV, separate Bose sound system and a sorely underused PlayStation 4. An oak topped coffee table sat in the centre of the room with three pull out drawers set beneath it, each filled with cables, documents and other paraphernalia that would be unsightly if left on display. The walls were coated in a mundane magnolia and the scattered frames on the walls held black and white photographs of skylines he had never visited.

In fact, if it wasn't for the two large oak bookcases that sandwiched the TV, a person would be hard pushed to find anything to signify a single person's interests or personality at all.

Chris was, by definition, a bachelor. Though the word itself seemed to instil some vision of a suave gentleman out living his best life, and that was not him.

The only child in a single parent family, he was raised by his mother after his father skipped out on them when she was six months pregnant. He had as normal a life as anyone could expect growing up, but when his mother began to suffer with Alzheimer's induced dementia around the time he turned thirty, he found himself acting as her carer; something that he in no way took to begrudgingly.

He'd had fifteen difficult years with her, practically a record for Alzheimer's sufferers, before she eventually passed leaving him to pick up his life again in his mid-forties.

His fork sank into the tuna on the plate, flaking smoothly as he brought it to his mouth. The remote in his left hand was still casually scrolling through the endless options available on the TV, determined to find something new and not fall into another rewatch of the same comfort shows.

Glancing casually at the open laptop on the coffee table, previously left on the Urb-Oboros forum page, he noticed a small red notification bubble along the top of the page. A new discussion.

Rich woke to the sound of nothing. His life wasn't guided by an alarm clock or anywhere to be. Business hours definitely didn't apply to him.

Kicking the sheets off, he sat up and stretched his arms skyward before stepping out of the bed. In his half-awakened stupor, he pinballed off the walls between the bed and the bathroom before reaching the toilet to urinate. After the lengthy stop-start stream of piss subsided he shook it vigorously as he was always annoyed by the few droplets that seemed to hang around just to darken a small area of his boxers.

He zombie shuffled back to the bedroom and picked up the t-shirt laying on the ground where he'd dropped it last night and threw it on before grabbing his phone from the bedside table.

9:24pm

Another win for his non-existent sleep pattern.

He was glad to see a lack of text messages or anything of an urgent nature to bother him but had several notifications for the Urbex forum. He was missing out on the action.

After heading downstairs he went straight to the kitchen and clicked the kettle on to boil before making his way to the fridge and taking a few large gulps straight from a carton of fresh orange juice. In the front room, he grabbed his laptop and fired it up to see what he was missing, dismissing multiple pop ups demanding updates before he could get to what he was doing.

He quickly found the new thread that detailed the next planned outing. It had already seen some interaction. He settled down on the sofa with the laptop on his knee to read the updates; the kettle boiling in the next room serving as a background soundtrack.

July 31st 2022: Hidden cave exploration

(18:20pm) **Francine_Nightcrawle1r(Admin):**
Hi folks, hope everyone is doing well. Back again with another Urb-Oboros adventure. I know the last one turned out to be a bit of a disappointment, but I'm hoping this will be a lot better. Through a stroke of perhaps fate, it has been brought to my attention that there is a cave hidden away in the Peak District, that looks to have been previously sealed up. I thought this coming Sunday would work as it gives everyone time to make arrangements, but also the weather looks to be scorching this weekend. FYI, I recommend bringing a towel and swimwear!

(18:34pm) **Spooky_Sophie666:**
Oooh Creepy! Aaron and I will definitely be there. And don't beat yourself up about the hostel, it was still a fun adventure.

(18:55pm) **KingKakarot:**
>Yeah we'll be there. Looks like a big place, but if it's not too far east, shouldn't be too bad.

(19:03pm) **KingKakarot:**
>I hope we have to drive through Tintwistle! Haha!

(19:36pm) **Dora.T.Explorer:**
>The pics Francine showed me looked really cool. Definitely a bit creepy.

(20:04) **Francine_Nightcrawler(Admin):**
>It is on the east side of things, so shouldn't be a bad drive at all. With the weather, be sure to pack refreshments though.

(20:05) **Francine_Nightcrawler(Admin):**
>And yes, you will drive through Tintwistle!

(20:20) **Spooky_Sophie666:**
>I'm already going through my bikini's! oh this is exciting.

(20:44) **Chris.Miller1975:**
>Good evening, all. This sounds great, I will for sure be in attendance. Caves are always great for photography, so I will make sure to bring my tripod too.

(21:17) **KingKakarot:**
>Chris, you are a tripod.

(21:18) **KingKakarot:**
>Wait. No. That's not what I meant.

(21:35) **Jack_of_Hearts:**
>I'm pretty sure I can make this one. Bit different to the usual locations.

(21:47) **Rich.By.Name:**
>Not exactly "urban" exploring though is it?

(22:10) **Spooky_Sophie666:**
>Rich! Don't be a asshole. It will be fun.

(22:13) **KingKakarot:**
>Yeah Richie Rich, don't be a fun sponge!

(22:15) **Rich.By.Name:**
>Nothing says urban like a natural rock formation. Calm down, I didn't say I wasn't coming.

(22:45) **Francine_Nightcrawler(Admin):**
>Rich, I hear what you're saying, but it looks to be a good location. I didn't want to say anything either, but it's not 'untouched' shall we say.

(23:10) **Rich.By.Name:**
>I'm just winding you up. It's cool, I'll be there.

(23:30) **Like_a_G6:**
>I'll be there. I'll dig out my camo bikini for Aaron.

(23:44) **Spooky_Sophie666:**
>I know you're joking Grace, but imma inbox you and talk swimwear!

(23:53) **Rich.By.Name:**
>Nobody needs to see my flabby arse in speedo's.

(00:15) **KingKakarot:**
Agreed!

(08:30) **Dora.T.Explorer:**
So exciting!

(09:38) **Francine_Nightcrawler(Admin):**
well if everyone is onboard with the location and date, I'll get sorted on directions and keep people in the loop.

(10:07) **Chris.Miller1975:**
I won't be bringing swimwear, but I look forward to it.

(11:05) **Like_a_G6:**
I'm picturing you in one of those red and white striped, all in one bathing suits from the seaside.

(13:34) **JustVictor:**
I do not think I can make it this time friends. So sorry.

(14:22) **Spooky_Sophie66:**
Oh Victor, that sucks. Much sadface.

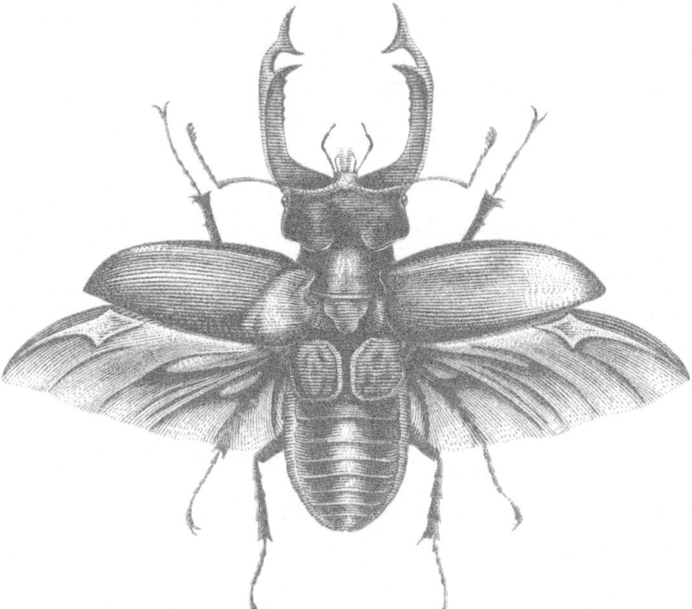

CHAPTER 8

July 31st, 2022

The high morning sun assaulted the roof of the red Micra as it turned onto the country lane, signalling that she was nearing the finish line of her journey.

Grace was thankful for the newly arrived coverage from the trees that ran along either side of the winding road, as she reached to drop the AC of her car down a couple of notches.

So far it had been a smooth drive, but the blistering heat wasn't something she was enjoying from her current position locked in this metallic sweat box with only a red bull to tide her over. The audiobook version of James Herbert's The Rats was keeping her company between the nasal interruptions from her satnav, *stay in the left lane and continue forward*, and while she wasn't making the best time, she certainly wasn't running too late.

She'd instantly regretted the decision to wear the bikini under her clothes as by the time she'd driven a couple of miles, two thirds of it were lodged firmly in her arse crack and it was difficult to extract a wedgie at seventy miles an hour.

As she continued around the narrow winding country road shrouded in trees, it eventually opened into fields and farmlands, and the glowing ball of fiery death once again began to make its presence known.

She drove past a few quaint little cottages as the rural area took on a slightly inhabited feel, complete with signs warning her to kill her speed. She wondered if this was sizeable enough to be classed as some tiny little village as images of a small schoolhouse and a solitary pub, complete with suspicious locals, filled her mind.

Leaving the 'village' behind her just as quickly as it arrived, she found herself again under the cover of forest as she picked up speed and settled in for the last leg of the drive.

Even without the squawking updates from her satnav, she'd have known she was closing in on her destination as she began to pass ramblers on the roadside. Small clusters of well-prepared people armed with water bottles and walking sticks in brightly coloured clothing and shoes, moving like animated pride flags against a backdrop of forest green.

At her satnav's request she made a left turn onto a narrow trail leading into the forest which was barely wide enough for a car, and she prayed that where would be nobody looking to leave through this route until she made it to her destination.

A tall pole was buried in the ground at the start of the junction with a hand carved wooden signpost nailed to its side, confirming this was the correct direction for Storm Vault Peak.

Thankfully reaching the end of the trail before encountering any oncoming traffic, she turned into the large dirt bowl that served as a carpark to the raucous applause of her welcoming party.

Grace parked up and headed over to them, a large blue water bottle swinging from her arm.

Jack staggered a little as Aaron cheered and waved his arms, from his vantage point seated on Jack's broad shoulders.

"Whoah, be careful, you tit,' he said as he bent at the knees to lower Aaron back to the ground.

Aaron hopped off his shoulders as he tucked his head down and wobbled for a few steps as he found his balance. "Sorry, mister muscles, I didn't think."

"Title of your autobiography," Sophie joked from her position leaning against the side of their car, a massive plume of cherry-scented smoke shrouding her as she vaped.

"Thanks, Grace," Jack called. "It's nice not to be the last to arrive for once."

She tilted into a majestic bow, rotating the open palm on her outstretched hand. "Glad I could be of service."

A cursory glance around the clearing told her she was in fact the last to arrive – Sophie and Francine leaned against the blue Kuga emitting clouds of sweet smelling fog, Rich sat half in, half out the back of the car swapping his trainers, Jack and Aaron appeared to be engaged in some sort of homo-erotic tussle, and Chris was away in the background already snapping photos of the forest.

"Victor definitely couldn't make it then?" Grace asked as she caught Francine's attention.

"Sadly not. He had to take his grandma to a hospital appointment, apparently, and he was insistent that we didn't reschedule while the weather was good."

"Good is subjective I suppose," Grace said as she swatted at something that had landed on her forearm, crushing it into a smear against her dark skin. "And no Dora?"

"Couldn't get her shift swapped," Francine replied.

"Maybe Dora and Victor are the same person. Has anyone ever seen them in the same room together?" Aaron joked.

Jack cuffed him on the ear as he approached from behind. "Other than the fact that one is a petite blonde girl, and the other is a timid Eastern European man, they were both at the last one," he said as he gave the girls a smile. "You're not doing much to defend that idiot status, mate."

"Oh. Yeah, I knew that. Are we ready to go see this cave anyway, I'm sweating my tits off here."

"I think we're good to go," Francine said as she heaved her Jansport backpack up onto her shoulder. "Double check you've all got your water bottles and stuff first, it's a bit of a hike."

They walked for nearly an hour, following the tread-worn paths of other hikers in a gradual ascent that was thankfully shrouded by the coverage of trees, shielding them from the direct assault of sunlight.

They stopped twice in this time to take short breaks and let Rich catch his breath and complain. *You know there are plenty of hiking groups I could have joined, this isn't what I signed up for.*

As they reached the crest of a hill, in which Rich again took measures to complain about the gradient, their vantage point of the area opened up to the expanse of forest to their right. Tall trees, grassy hills and a nervous system of streams and brooks that branched throughout the woods. To their immediate left as the hill dropped, the forest continued more densely to the left, hugging the staggering sandstone mountain that reached to the heavens before them.

With the directions memorized, Francine took the others down the beaten track, and they made their way through lesser chartered territory into the dense forest, keeping the mountain to their right as they worked their way around. The foliage closed in tightly around them and made it feel much later in the day as they wove between trees in the dim light.

The scent in the air was a mixture of the musty damp soil beneath their feet and the heady pine aroma of the tall conifer trees that surrounded them. Occasional breaks in the tightly packed tree formations allowed enormous spotlights of sun to break through and the humid air here was claylike and powdery, dust motes danced in the sun's rays in these pockets of daylight alongside tiny insects rhythmically hovering in the warmth.

As they continued, the wind began to whistle through the trees, bringing with it a stronger earthy smell and a cool refreshing reprieve from the heat.

Rich stopped for a second as the breeze passed over him and surveyed the area around him thoughtfully. "Do you guys hear that?" he asked as he waited for the group to stop.

"What?" Sophie asked as her head darted about the area, nose in the air like a meerkat.

"Exactly," he said as he pulled at the front of his t-shirt, taking this time to attempt to cool off. "It's gone silent. There are no birds, no rustling in the trees, it's like all the sounds around us have been swallowed up."

Everyone began to look around the small clearing they had found themselves in, though nobody was quite sure what they were looking for. Searching for visible signs of the absence of noise was a slightly redundant exercise.

"It is a little eerie, I will admit," Chris said through the lens of his camera as he took the time to snap more shots of the local flora and its absence of fauna. "The whole forest can't be densely packed with life, though. Maybe the birds are all just high in the trees enjoying the sun."

Rich shivered as if unease was coursing through him, an ironic thing for one who had made keeping others at a healthy arm's length his business.

"It's just quiet." Aaron joined in. "We're in a forest and nobody is about, big whoop. Let's just get to this cave."

"As always, I hate to agree with Aaron," Francine said before winking at Sophie. "But he's not wrong. We're in the middle of nowhere, I don't think it's cause for alarm."

"How much further is it?" Sophie asked.

"Probably another half hour or so I'd say. Not too far."

Jack took a huge gulp of water from his bottle. "Let's crack on then."

Twenty minutes later they found themselves at a sparsely wooded area, the tree's having gradually thinned out as they drew closer to the side of the huge rockface.

Rich faced what looked to have once been a large cave entrance in the side of the mountain, now packed with slabs of stone and rubble filling most of the opening. A small area, just larger than that of a grown man, was open to the lower right side of the entrance, and slabs of rock scattered around the ground before them where it had clearly come loose.

This is where people come to find a sticky end. Rich thought as he glanced into the dark tunnel entrance.

A warm breeze emanated from the hole, carrying a moist, damp odour as it washed over them.

"Here we are," Francine announced as she threw her hands up in the air.

Rich and Aaron simultaneously dropped to the ground, relief filling their faces as they reveled in being sat down for the time being.

"That is creeeepy," Sophie said as she drew out her phone and zoomed in on the cave entrance.

Grace and Jack moved to join Aaron and Rich on the ground as they watched Chris drop to a knee and begin framing more shots with his camera.

"Nearly noon," Grace said, checking her phone. "Not bad really."

"Feels much later." Red-faced and sweaty, Rich drained the rest of the water from his drinking bottle.

Aaron lay back and watched the clouds slowly pass in the sky above him through a border of leafy trees. "It better be the coolest cave I've ever seen, that's for sure. We're talking genie-in-a-lamp-cool."

"Oh yeah, what would your three wishes be, mate?" Jack asked.

"Ooh okay." He sat back up an excited look on his face. "Rich, obviously."

"I'm overrated," Rich interjected with a grin.

"Fuck off, money rich I mean." Aaron replied.

Also overrated, Rich said under his breath.

"Second," he paused. "Teleporting. I'm lazy. And last…" he jerked his head and eyebrows in tandem towards Sophie. "Bigger tits," he said as he made grabby hands in front of his own chest with a smirk.

"Pig," Grace said as she flung a branch from the ground his way. "Also, if you're rich you can just pay for those, why waste a wish?"

Aaron gave her a huge smile before answering. "I'm rich with a big titty goth girlfriend, what else do I need?"

Jack and Rich burst into laughter, drawing Sophie's attention as Grace rolled her eyes.

"Men. You really are simple beings."

"Guilty." Jack raised his hand in the air.

"What am I missing?" Sophie said as she came see what was going on.

"Oh, nothing much, Aaron was just telling us how much he loves your tits," Grace said.

"Aaron!" she snapped as her cheeks flushed.

Francine arrived shortly after with Chris on her heels and they sat and joined the conversation, suggesting they all take this time to eat and get rested before they headed into the cave.

Rich couldn't shake the background anxiety that was beginning to gnaw at his brain. Something just didn't feel right, but he couldn't place it.

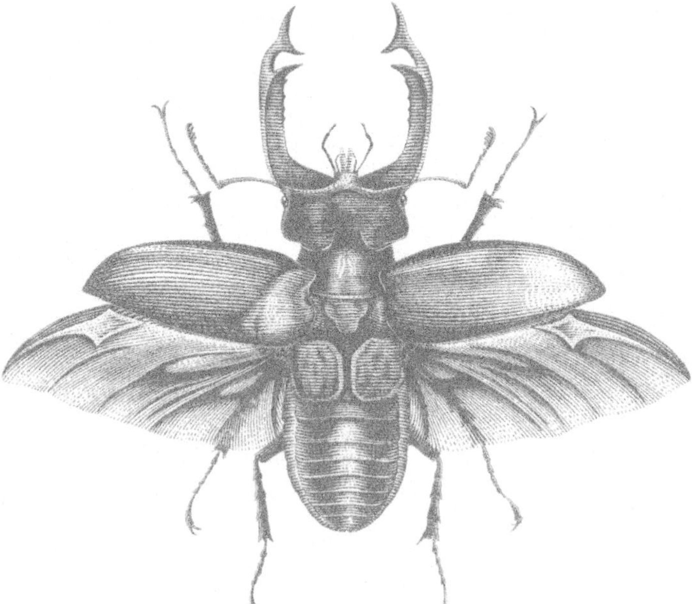

CHAPTER 9

Sophie sat on the ground moving the phone around her face as she used the camera screen to check her make-up wasn't running. She had taken great lengths to apply everything that was waterproof, knowing she had a pool to look forward to later. She'd spent a lot of time picking out her swimming costume for today's trip as she had resigned herself to the idea that ghosts in a cave wasn't very likely. In part, she agreed with Rich that this wasn't really urban exploration, but it still seemed like it would be fun and old caves could be pretty creepy.

Chris sat with Jack as he scrolled through the wealth of photos that he'd taken so far, stopping occasionally to narrate how the light was just perfect in certain shots. Jack did his best to look interested, but he knew that this was his fate for being polite. He knew that Chris was fully aware that his attempts to show Aaron or Rich would be met with ridicule.

The others found themselves filling the time with light-hearted small talk and jokes. It was fair to say that while this was a regular gathering of people, they didn't actually know a great deal about each other and their personal lives.

A shadow moved across the group darkening the skies as the clouds above shifted to block out the sun and the breeze started to pick up a little, giving a repeat reprieve from the heat.

They looked up in unison as the heavens opened and rain began to heavily pour down, pelting them with a ferocity that while refreshing in this heat, was somewhat alarming.

"Shit," Rich said as jumped up off the ground. "Bit of warning next time, God."

One by one they scrambled to their feet as the torrential downpour assaulted them.

"Break time's over then," Francine said as she darted in the direction of the cave. "Come on."

Needing no further direction, they all shot after her and slid one by one into the hole in the rock seeking to find shelter, Jack waiting to let each person squeeze through ahead of him before he brought up the rear.

Stepping inside, the first thing that hit Francine was the staggering humidity from the cave. The very air was heavy around them, and their now rain-soaked clothes clung to their bodies like the full body discomfort of a wet sock inside a shoe.

The only light source in this area was the jagged hole behind them and the torchlights on phones quickly began to blink into life as they raised them up, casting elongated human shadows across the rough sandstone walls.

"Everyone stays close while we're moving forward," Francine called out from the front. "I'm sure it's safe enough, but I don't want anyone breaking their neck while we're in the arse end of nowhere."

The mouth of the cave was about fifteen feet wide, slightly over that in height and looked to carry on a fair distance as the flashlights couldn't penetrate far enough to see the end of the tunnel.

They moved forward slowly, casting light around them as they took in their surroundings, the ceiling of the cave was layered with rough looking stalactites hanging down like the gaping maw of a giant creature above them.

"Stalactites," Aaron said proudly. "Because they hang tight from the ceiling."

Rich snorted. "Gold star. You're as learned as a thirteen-year-old."

"Hung like one too." Grace joined in.

"Alright. Fuck off the pair of you."

As they carried on along the tunnel it began to close in slightly around them, leaving enough room to pass through, but all the same feeling very claustrophobic. Francine wasn't exactly bothered by confined spaces, but she did feel somewhat smothered by the closeness of the walls, the feeling of being so confined making the air feel even heavier and restricting.

They felt themselves being slowly curved to the left as the cave continued and Francine realized that she could no longer see the light from the cave mouth behind them.

"Has anyone seen Descent?" Grace asked from her position in the middle of the train.

"I love that movie," Sophie piped up. "It's dead unsettling and tense."

"It's also shit-your-pants scary," Jack said. "But I get where your head's at, Grace."

"Yeah, except were not descending are we, so it's sort of irrelevant," said Aaron.

"Scary movie in a cave is still a scary movie in a cave. though. That's what I'm getting at. This is just feeling a bit murderous right now."

"Ruh roh, are you sca-wed of the dark?" Aaron said in a taunting toddler's voice.

"Laugh all you want, I think we all know if this was a horror movie, I'm the first to die."

Chris cleared his throat as he began to break the self-imposed silence he always found himself in whenever the group got talking as a whole. "Not necessarily, I think movies have come on a long way in recent years and Hollywood is trying to quash the old stereotypes that we're so used to." He paused for a second to decide whether to continue and then carried on. "I think Jordan Peele has done a lot to really broaden the scope of what we expect from movies in the recent years."

"Maybe, but ultimately if you run an entirely Black cast, the first person to die is still going to be a Black guy, technically," Rich said.

"For fuck's sake, guys. I'm just saying it's creepy. Christ."

"Well, I'm not strictly white, so maybe I'll die first," Francine called back from the head of the group.

"This is a weird thing to pull the race card on." Rich laughed.

The passage continued veering further to the left before it straightened up and began to wind off to the right. As they moved along, the humidity increased and the air became stuffy, bringing with it an earthy, mildew-like odour that filled their nostrils. The walls of the cave, that had closed in even further, were coated with dark green algae and were damp to the touch, beads of water glistened against the glow from their phones as they passed.

The tunnel eventually began to widen as they proceeded further along, and the delicate sounds of water dripping rhythmically could be heard ahead of them as they reached the end of the passage.

From the front of the procession Francine stopped abruptly and gasped at the view ahead of her.

The tunnel opened into a huge cave of easily a hundred feet wide and about ten feet high. the walls of the cave were coated in algae and had vine-like plants and greenery covering a good portion of its surface. The ceiling was again covered in sporadic patches of stalactites but had a huge circular hole in the middle that allowed sunlight to descend into the cave like a giant spotlight, casting its glow across the area below.

In the centre of the cave was a massive body of water that looked as close to a man-made pool as anyone could ask for, and she took a moment to marvel at the true miracle of nature.

The calm waters had the faintest sway about them and were lit up by the sunlight from above to glow in the most beautiful hues of green that she assumed were cast from the greenery on the surrounding cave walls. It looked surprisingly serene and seemed closer to a natural spring than a stagnant pool. In fact, with how humid it was in this domed cavern, it felt more like a sauna.

Francine paused for a moment on the threshold and felt a sense of relief wash over her. This was a great find, and she knew they'd think so too, washing the bad taste of the less than impressive hostel visit out of their mouths.

"Come on, stop hogging the view." Aaron gently pushed on Francine's back. "Is it cool?"

She stepped forward, dropping down a couple of feet into the actual cave, allowing the rest of the group to spill out behind her amid a mix of gasps.

"It's like a hidden grotto," Sophie exclaimed as she stepped from the tunnel, eyes wide in wonder.

"Very cool." Grace agreed.

The party moved into the cavern and began to fan out, exploring the depths of the cave, the sound of Chris's camera clicks serving as the soundtrack to their search.

Rich moved to a large slab of stone about two feet in height and sat himself down, running the pointed toe of his shoe over what looked to be a pile of long rotted wood and rope that had fused and compacted with years of neglect, on the ground before him. "I'm not too proud to eat my words," he said, directing his attention towards Francine. "It's not very urban, but I have to admit this is really cool. I can't believe this has lay untouched for so long."

"Literal party central, right?" Aaron seconded from his place in the middle of the cave staring up through the hole in the ceiling.

"I'm glad it passes inspection," Francine said, her whole body awash with the warm fuzzy feeling of success. The disappointment of the previous excursion was already beginning to feel like a distant memory.

Chris cleared his throat loudly from his position beside Aaron. "Come and take a look at this."

"What is it?" Francine asked as she stepped over to the pair, leaving her backpack on the ground against the rock by Rich.

Chris pointed to the large hole above them and swirled his finger in a circle expressively. "There looks to be symbols and gems or something set around the hole. Look."

This drew the attention of Jack and Sophie who moved to join them.

"Hang on," Chris said as he snapped another photo before flipping the camera around and finding the picture on the screen.

They all crowded around the camera as he zoomed to the area around the hole.

"What is that?" Jack said as he watched the picture begin to focus.

Around the north and south of the hole there looked to be carved images of an eagle with a snake grasped in its talons. The east and west had crude lightning bolts carved into the stone and offset between each symbol was a large green gemstone embedded in the rock.

"Oh wow, that is some witchy, culty shit," Sophie said as they looked from the screen up to the actual hole above them.

"I told you there were some surprises." Francine beamed.

Their focus on the symbols was soon broken by a loud splash from behind them.

Spinning around Francine saw Grace break through the surface of the pool, droplets of water clung to her short, dark hair, shimmering in the sunlight like fresh dew on grass. Her clothing lay in a pile on the other side of the cave, heaped on top of each other like a person had been vaporized.

"Damn, this is incredible. You guys need to hurry up and get in here," she said as she waded on the spot, grinning from ear to ear.

"On it," Aaron said, already shirtless as he hopped on one foot pulling the shoe off the other and chucking it to the ground beside him in a frantic flurry of disrobing.

Jack shrugged at Sophie and Francine. "Can't fault the woman's logic."

Francine bobbed in the water beside Grace and Sophie as Aaron once again cannonballed into the pool sending a wave up around him and splashing over them as they shielded their faces against the tiny tsunami.

The pool seemed to sink over ten feet at the deepest points, and everyone took great delight in diving under and enjoying the cool waters about them.

The three girls had come readily equipped with their bikinis under their clothes and looked as at home here as they would at any beach. Jack and Aaron wore swim shorts of black and green respectively and while Jack was happy to swim in the waters, Aaron found repeatedly diving into the pool to be a much better use of his time.

Rich, who seemed happy to just submerge in the water, elbows resting on the edge of the pool, wore large red swim shorts that came down to his knees and had retained the t-shirt he was wearing. He clearly wasn't as comfortable in his own body as the rest of the group.

"Are you sure we can't convince you to take a dip, Chris?" he asked from the edge of the pool. "It's surprisingly warm in here."

Chris looked up from his vantage point behind his camera, seated on the rock that Rich had been perched on earlier and shook his head. It was clear to Francine that Chris didn't feel comfortable with the idea, and while they didn't exactly want to force him, she could tell they were feeling bad for him being left out sat on the sidelines. He was often the butt of their jokes, but it was all in jest, with no malice, and they didn't want him to feel excluded from the group too much.

"No, you guys have fun. I'm happy just getting some good shots in here. It really is a fantastic location."

"Suit yourself," Rich said as he sucked in a lung full of air and plunged himself under the water.

Before long everyone was fully submerged and swimming about in the waters, exploring the bottom for anything of interest and coming up with nothing more than sludge and different varieties of plant life. The heat inside the cavern was easily a few degrees warmer than it was outside, and the humidity added a greenhouse level of warmth into the mix, making the cool water a perfect temperature to kick back and relax in.

At Aaron's suggestion Sophie found herself sat on his shoulders while Grace in turn mounted Jack's, the foursome facing off in submerged gladiatorial combat, each trying to topple the other into the water. Rich had retired back to the edge of the pool, his now soaked blonde hair hanging in his face as he enjoyed the cooling effects of being drenched.

Francine was once again deep diving under the water, swimming about the pool while avoiding getting too close to the guy's war games.

At least they're all having fun.

Looking up through the water, she saw that the sunlight cascading through the open hole above was magnified and cast rainbows of colour across its surface. As she swam a little further along, her attention was drawn by movement from the corner of her eye.

Through the blurred surface of the water she saw what appeared to be the outline of a figure leaning forward to investigate the pool. The feminine form had flowing white hair that shimmered in the sunlight and through the lens of water, and the mostly exposed flesh looked an icy blue.

She froze on the spot as the cold finger of fear ran down her spine, starting from her neck and sending a ripple of dread through her whole body.

As she focused on the figure above her, the woman's head snapped left in a sudden jerky motion, the pinprick black pupils of her eyes locking on Francine's as her delicate features became clear. The eyes were mostly stark white sclera with the smallest inky dots in the centre, her skin was smooth, its features soft and almost ageless. Her prominent cheekbones raised as her lips drew back into a smile, the whiteness of her teeth amplified against the bubblegum pink of her gums.

Deep in the grip of terror, she realized the breath she had been holding had run its course and, in a panic, kicked her feet and rose to the surface, breaking through the water with a gasp as fresh oxygen filled her lungs.

Between gulps of air, she darted her head about searching for the mystery figure. The only person outside the pool was Chris, who seeing her panicked expression, rushed to the water's edge to see if she was alright.

"Francine are you alright?" he barked with a fine balance of panic and urgency.

She swam to the edge of the pool and flopped unceremoniously over the side and rolled onto the rough cave floor, breathing heavily as she lay on her back.

"There... there was someone there," she coughed. "a woman was looking into the water at me."

The commotion had drawn the attention of the rest of the group, and they too moved to the edge of the pool, Sophie jumping out to rush to Francine's aid.

"What? I've been out here the whole time, there's been nobody here but us," Chris said as he dropped to a knee at her side.

"Yeah, and with the exception of Grace faceplanting the water just now, we've all been above the surface, there's nobody else here." Jack cut in.

"I didn't just fucking make it up, Jack," Francine barked, her head spinning.

Sophie stroked Francine's shoulder as she continued to freak out. "Tell us what you saw?"

"It was a woman. She had white hair; it was almost like silk. And she looked blue, but it could have just been the water."

"You're describing Smurfette."

"Shut the fuck up, Aaron," Sophie snapped.

"I know what I saw, she smiled at me, but it was ... I don't know, really sinister."

"Francine, we're not saying you're making it up," Grace said. "You were under the water for a while, though, it could have been a weird hallucination. I don't know, can lack of oxygen do that?"

They were all silent for a while as Francine continued to take deep gasps of air and look bewildered.

"None of you saw anything?" she said after a while, her eyes darting around the cave. "Really?"

"Nothing," Chris confirmed as he took in the panic on Francine's face.

"I don't think any of us would be so calm or questioning of you if we had, hun," Rich said as he started to lift himself out of the water with a grunt. "Trick of the light or what Grace said, I don't know, but you're okay, and there's really nobody else here."

Even with Francine calmed down, the mood of the day had shifted, and everyone decided to leave the pool and towel off before getting dressed and gathering on dry land to relax. The cave was still pleasantly warm, and the sun shone down into the pool from above, hypnotically reflecting its rays across the gentle ripple of water.

"So, what do you think this was used for, then?" Rich asked the group.

"Huh?" Aaron said from his spot laying on the ground with his head in Sophie's lap.

"I mean, the cave itself seems natural enough, but with those gems and symbols around that opening, it was obviously used by people at some point."

"I have no clue," Francine said. "But I'm definitely going to do some research when we get back, see what I can dig up on this place." Her legs were still shaking, but she kept her voice bright and casual. No point bringing down the mood of the group. "Chris, can you send me those pictures you've taken in here?"

"of course. I was going to just upload them to the forum, that way the others can see as well."

"Perfect. That works."

"I'll get them up tonight when we get back. I'm glad I decided to go with digital today."

"Speaking of," Jack said. "Should we think about making a move? It's a fair hike back to the cars again."

"Yeah, you're probably right. It should be cooler now at least," Rich said.

"Especially as we're sopping wet," Sophie agreed.

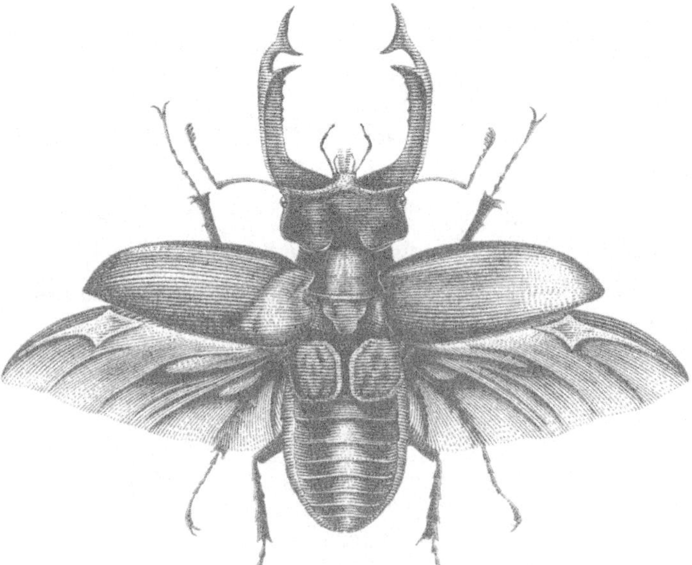

CHAPTER 10

After an equally tiring hike back through the forest, the group were still buzzing from the day's adventure, even with the slight air of unease from Francine's outburst. They reached the cars and said their goodbyes before piling into their vehicles.

Still wearing the same t-shirt he'd been swimming in, Rich sat in the back of the Ford with a towel under him, covering the back of the seat, the not entirely unpleasant pond smell clinging to him and filling the inside of the car. Aaron and Sophie in the front, having made sure to remove their clothes before swimming, didn't have such a strong aroma of the pool about them, but between the three, packed into such an enclosed space, there was a general mustiness to the air.

Though the early summer's evening should still be bright, with hours yet until sunset, they travelled with their backs to a storm. The slate grey skies spread behind them, creeping like looming death on their heels.

The car travelled casually along Baxter Street, and Rich noticed an eerie emptiness to the neighbourhood as people fled inside to avoid the wall of rain that was now present alongside the blanket of deep grey clouds above them. Aaron slowed the car as he turned into the cul-de-sac on their right, a horseshoe of about twelve grand homes sat with their pristine gardens and immaculately clean brickwork.

"I still can't believe this is where you live," Aaron said as he cruised slowly along, eyeballing all the homes he could never afford. "I guess Richie Rich is a pretty apt nickname."

Rich's face soured for a moment, the grimace disappearing as fast as it had arrived, as he cleared his throat. "Just know if you plan on stepping in on my turf, there will be hell to pay," he said in an approximation of an old Hollywood gangster. "The west side is mine and mine alone."

"Dude, I think Sophie would make a more believable drug lord than you."

"I could be a drug lord," she piped up. "Well, drug lady I suppose, though that doesn't sound right, does it? A drug lady sounds like a strung out headcase begging for her next hit."

"Hi, I'm a drug lady," Rich said in a squeaky voice as they all began to giggle like children.

The car came to a halt outside Rich's house, and he quickly thanked them again for the lift, passing them a twenty for fuel as he opened the door and began to step out.

"Rich," Aaron called after him. "Great deflection. You keep your secrets," he said with a smile as their eyes met.

"Okay, Frodo. Thanks again and drive safe, guys."

THE WHITE PLASTIC CLOCK ON THE KITCHEN WALL SHOWED ten forty-five as Francine, phone in hand, paced the kitchen.

The short distance from the car to the front door of her modest home had been enough to soak her to the bone, and she'd quickly stripped off and jumped into a pair of ninja turtle lounge pants and a black vest top, oversized monster slippers buried her feet in a world of plush green fabric and black fur as she paced the tiled floor.

"Did you see the photo's Chris uploaded to the forum yet?" she said into the mouthpiece as she began the task of finding sustenance. The almost ritualistic act of opening and closing cupboards that she knew didn't contain anything of worth, in hope that some magical food fairy had deposited supplies while her back was turned.

"I did," came the tinny voice of Dora through the phone's speakers. "It looked so cool, gutted I had to miss it. Maybe we can go back again sometime."

There was a hesitant pause as the day's events quickly flashed through Francine's mind, causing her a momentary shiver. "Yeah, I think people would be up for that. Did you see the crazy symbols and gems around the ceiling? So bizarre."

"Yeah. So weird. I wonder what went on up there back whenever they were done."

"Same." Francine rifled through drawers in the freezer. "I've been trying to research some history on the place, but all I'm getting when I google Storm Vault Peak are articles about some crazy guy in prison who apparently ranted about it during his trial."

"Oh wow, did he kill people up there or something?"

"I haven't done a deep dive yet, but I doubt it. I'd imagine access wouldn't have been so easy for a murder site. I'm definitely going to look into that though if I don't find much else. Anyway, how was your day?"

She listened attentively as Dora recounted her day for her, being sure to add the occasional grunts of confirmation where appropriate as she dug out a frozen ready meal from the freezer – chicken tikka masala, forty minutes in the oven, that would suffice. This was obviously the bare bones of a meal that really required other accompaniments, but she just didn't have the energy. She'd had far more simplistic meals in her life.

After bumping the freezer door shut with her hip, she moved across to the oven and spun the dial as the light inside flared to life and the ascending hum of the fan began to whirr. She dropped the frozen meal down on the kitchen counter and fished a knife out of the drawer of cutlery and began to stab at the plastic covering on the container, not really paying attention to Dora's words about her day.

Francine shimmied along the front of the countertop to the sink and dropped the knife into the basin and flipped up the handle as water started to pour from the tap.

She glanced out the window as the rain hammered down in the darkness, her own reflection filling the glass, and as a bolt of lightning flashed in the sky, lighting up her garden it briefly illuminated a dark form in the distance.

"Babe," she said as she tried to peer out into the dark. "I'm going to have to call you back, I think there's something in the garden." Her stomach filled with butterflies.

"What? Something like a person?"

"I'm not sure what I saw, but I'm going to go check it out."

"It's pissing down out there. Be careful, okay?"

"of course, don't worry. I'll call you back in a bit."

She ended the call and placed her phone down on the countertop before moving to the backdoor and sliding the silver bolt across the top of it with a click, then unlocking the actual door and pulling it open as she was met with an immediate misting of rain and the cool night air.

The long, narrow garden tapered away from her, tall wooden fences providing a barrier between neighbouring houses. The limited rows of concrete paving at the back of the house quickly gave way to a garden that was predominantly lawn, with a solitary wooden shed, in a dilapidated state, at the far corner.

The only source of light came from the kitchen window that looked out onto the garden, casting its glow far enough to provide some semblance of visibility.

Set most of the way down the lawn stood a hooded figure, statue still in the centre of the grass, seemingly unfazed by the rain that washed over them, their gaze levelled towards the floor as the sopping wet hood drooped down masking the face of this unknown person.

As Francine stood frozen in the doorway, the figure turned and slowly began to amble along the lawn towards her, its movements weary and wavering. She couldn't help but think of their movements like the exhausted stagger of many a final girl, limping to safety after the explosive climax to a great slasher movie.

The figure had closed half the gap between them before Francine broke free of the stupor she'd found herself in. Watching this person creep slowly towards her, Francine called out into the darkness.

"I don't know who you are, or why you're in my garden, but I suggest you head back the way you came in," she said, though as soon as the words left her lips, she had to wonder where it was that they had entered from.

When this didn't have the desired effect, she continued with as much authority as she could muster, "I will call the police if you don't get lost." As panic set in, she found herself transfixed with this approaching form. Every cell in her body screamed at her to slam the door, lock it and grab the closest pointy implement she could find, but still she watched on as they drew closer.

With less than a dozen feet between them the figure came to a halt, raised both hands to their hood, delicate pale fingers gripping the sides of the rain-soaked fabric, and began to draw it back.

THE MAN'S HEAD LIFTED CLEANLY FROM HIS BODY AS EASILY as the stem being plucked from an apple, six inches of spine coming with it as blood bloomed from the jagged stump of his neck. The lifeless head was held briefly in the ninja's grasp before being forcefully thrown at the still standing, decapitated body.

"Fatality," Jack echoed in tandem with the voice on his computer screen, the games controller gripped tightly in his hands.

He'd arrived home and immediately headed straight for the shower to wash both the sweat and pond stink off himself before throwing on some grey joggers and collapsing on the couch. The idea of heading to the gym was there, as it always was, but he reasoned that the legwork he'd put in on their trip would suffice as his exercise for the day.

An evening of vegetating on the couch playing games wouldn't hurt him, and he had to admit it was something he didn't allow himself the time for nearly as often as he should. His gym routine was all-encompassing at times, and there was a level of self-imposed guilt he levelled at himself for sitting round and relaxing. Many people had joked at it being a little obsessive, and perhaps they were right, but he couldn't switch it off.

The images on the screen began to fade to black as the overlay of blood splattered across it and dripped down slowly, readying itself to load into the next battle. For a few brief seconds the screen was totally black, and Jack could see himself reflected, though his image was wildly distorted.

He stared in horror at the bloated stomach that hung over the top of his sweatpants, bulbous and coated in a layer of body hair. His arms, still gripping the controller, were chubby and reminded him of a toddler's fat little limbs and an almost unrecognizable face stared back at him, jowly and worn, the lips cracked and dry.

A wave of nausea rushed over him, and he threw the controller across the room as he jumped up off the couch in a panic, patting himself down and moving to look at his reflection in the mirror above the fireplace.

Everything was as it should be. He took slow, steady breaths as he tried to get his heartrate back under control, having broken out in a cold sweat at the sight of his earlier reflection. The game had moved on from its loading darkness and the two combatants filled the screen, face to face ready for combat.

He crossed the room and picked up the controller from the ground and exited the game back to the home screen. Whatever trick his mind had just played on him had absolutely killed his desire to relax. Perhaps he could make time to visit the gym after all.

"Tink?"

Francine's eyes widened in shock as she watched the hood fall back from the stranger's head, revealing a familiar face. A decade more aged than last she saw it, but recognizable none the less.

"Tink, what the fuck? What are you doing here? How are you even here?" her stomach churned as she ran through memories of the past. Memories that felt like a lifetime ago, but as she was now finding out, still felt as fresh and raw as they had back then.

Tink slowly stepped forward, bridging the gap between them as the rain continued to lash down around them, soaking them both to the bone. Her pale features, now weathered with age lines, were partly hidden under the long dark hair that was plastered to her face but beneath it a smile began to grow across her face.

"Frannie, it's good to see you." She reached out and enveloped her in a strong, damp embrace.

Francine stood frozen in place and let the woman hug her, arms limp at her side. She had no idea what was going on and felt caught in the twilight zone.

"Look, this is insane, but can we maybe take this indoors and out of the rain?" Francine said, her heart pounding as she pulled free from the hug and stepped back towards the house as Tink followed.

Back in the kitchen, Francine stood in a small puddle of water as she took in the person before her. Tink looked on with a cock of her head, as if patiently waiting for the onslaught of questions that were to come. Even with the toll of years visible in the lines of her face and the dark circles under her eyes, it was unmistakably Tink.

Except it wasn't.

The initial shock and panic had passed, and Francine wasn't an idiot. While this looked exactly like her first love in the flesh, Tink had walked out on her years ago, and if what she said was true, she'd left the country. So, there was no way she'd just turned up a decade later to stand around in her garden in the pissing rain.

The blood in her veins was ice water, and it wasn't from the cold. She forced down a shiver and began to mentally strengthen herself.

"What's brought you back then?" She spoke as calmly as she could, attempting to put a small amount of snark into it as her eyes scanned the room for a weapon.

"To see you of course," she said as she tiptoed forward in an almost seductive manner. "It's been so long. So, so long, Frannie."

"You'll forgive me if I don't buy it though, right? Tink walked away with no concern for anyone other than herself, and that was a long time ago. You seriously expect me to believe she's just turned up outside my home in the dark after so long? Never mind the concept of even knowing where I was." Francine's eyes landed on the knife submerged in the basin of the sink.

The Tink simulacrum continued to close the gap as she gave Francine a hurt look. "Is it so hard to believe that I wanted to see you again? I've missed you greatly, your voice, your touch, your lips."

"You haven't missed me," Francine spat. "Because you've never fucking met me." Francine stepped to her left and pulled the wet kitchen knife from the sink before spinning to brandish it at the woman.

"Oh …" A cruel smile filled the woman's face. "I wouldn't say that."

Francine watched as the woman transformed before her eyes. The dark hair quickly became white as if its ink was being washed away, and her features began to shift and tighten as they reformed. The fleshy hue of her skin shifted to a pale grey and Francine gasped as her pupils drew in like tiny black holes, whitening the rest of the eyes. The woman from the cave stood before her, still flashing that hideous grin.

The woman lunged forward to grab at Francine, who swung the knife before burying it deep into the monster's side. Unfazed by the attack, the woman swiped down and knocked Francine's hand free from the slick knife handle and pinned her against the kitchen counter, fingers digging in tightly to her arms.

"Now, now, there's really no need to struggle, dear."

Francine thrashed helplessly trying to break free of the vice-like grip she was being held in as the putrid stench of pond water on the woman's breath hit her as her mouth opened and moved towards hers. An overwhelming coolness emanated from her body, and it was like being stood just a little too close to an open freezer. The chill did nothing to settle the rising fear inside Francine.

The woman's mouth pressed roughly over hers and she felt the cool flesh against her lips, locked in a lovers embrace. Still struggling to break free, she managed to twist her arm and reach the handle of the blade, still embedded in the woman's ribs, and began to twist.

The woman emitted a slight moan into Francine's mouth and then pushed harder in a passionate, unreciprocated kiss. With a sudden burst of vicious strength and ferocity, the woman's grip on Francine's arms started to tighten and nails dug into her flesh. She tried to turn her head away from the embrace and the immediate agony hit her as both arms snapped under the sudden force of the woman's hands. The flesh below Francine's elbows ruptured as splintered bones pierced outwards through the skin.

The woman released her grip from Francine's limp, lifeless arms and brought her hands up to grasp her head, pulling her back into the kiss.

Pain coursed through Francine's body and tears rolled down her cheeks as she remained pinned mouth to mouth with her attacker. A tide of foul-tasting water began to fill her mouth and she started to gag, terror taking over as her eyes widened and she continued to thrash. The water continued to flow with increased pressure, and she could feel it being forced down her throat as she choked.

On the far side of the room, the phone on the counter began to vibrate wildly on the table as the screen lit up the kitchen. Francine wanted to scream.

Dora calling back to check in.

Francine continued swallowing the fountain of water as the reality of her imminent death started to sink in. Both pain and pressure were beginning to build up inside her and her body felt bloated and tight, ready to burst like overripe fruit and she didn't know how long she could hold out, staring into the blank eyes of the woman pinning her.

Unbearable agony wracked her body as she felt her flesh rupturing under the pressure, and the sickening tearing of skin was the last thing she heard before losing consciousness.

The woman released her grip on Francine's head and let her body fall like dead weight onto the ground as she turned to look at the phone, still buzzing away on the countertop.

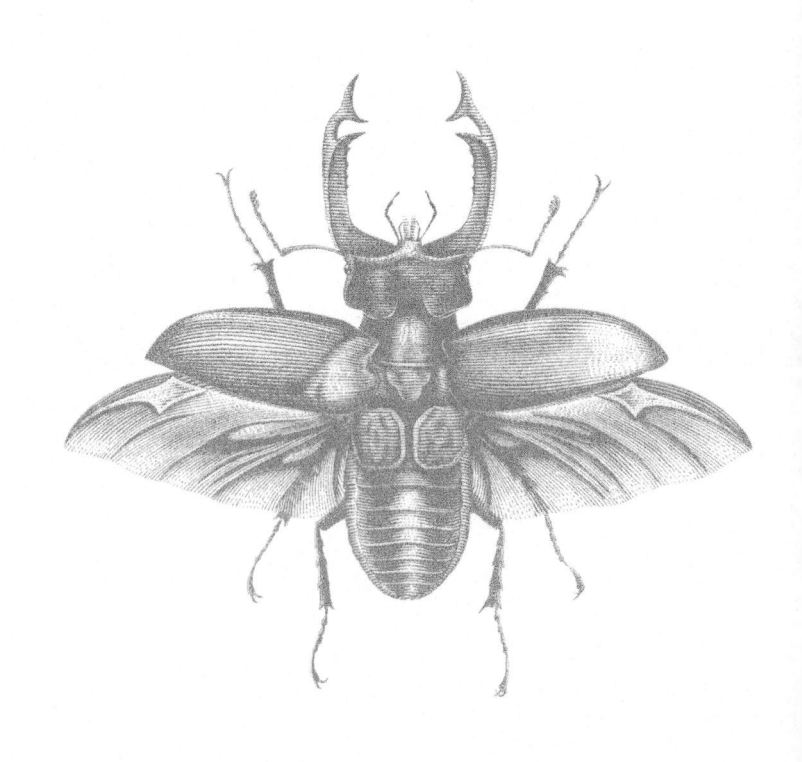

CHAPTER 11

As she lay on the bed basking in the post-sex afterglow, her flesh still clammy and refreshing in the much-welcomed coolness of the night, Grace glanced at the man sharing her bed. He lay on his back, fingers clasped behind his head, the silky emerald sheets draped over his lower body covering his modesty as he shifted his leg from under them to take advantage of the cool air.

She nudged his taut, athletic frame with the back of her fist gently. "Say something nice."

He gave her a puzzled look before answering, "What?"

"I've just let you inside me, say something nice to me."

"Let me?" he laughed. "I didn't realise this was some sort of gift. And it's hardly the first time, is it?"

Grace rolled onto her side and tucked a fist under her cheek as she gave him a wide-eyed pout. "You know what I mean, just humour me."

"Fine," he said as he drew in a breath and let it out slowly as his eyes moved about the room. "I never thought in all my days I'd share a bed with a face that could launch a thousand ships."

"Eugh. I take it back." Her tongue pushed past her teeth in a gag.

"Your arse is superb, too," he offered.

"Okay, that's a bit better." She leaned down and kissed him gently on the chest.

She sat up in the bed, the cool faux- leather of the headboard a wonderful chill on her back and glanced lazily around the room.

A modest set up by any means. The TV mounted on the wall was placed above a small bookcase situated below it, which was in turn sandwiched between an Ikea entry level wardrobe and chest of drawers. Her sunburst bass guitar, rested against the far wall alongside a heaped washing basket.

I'm living like a teenager.

She didn't like to linger too long on her current living situation as it became a quick downward spiral into the many failings of her life up to this point. A single bedroom in a four-person house share, a job, that while it paid the bills, wasn't exactly going to help her reach heights beyond her current status, and the occasional gig in venues that seemingly pumped week-old body odour in through the air vents. Not even a modest living really.

Too late. There it was – the spiralling. Twenty-four years of age, another orphan of the care system. It was a surprise to nobody that the little Black girl failed to find a good home or a loving new family.

It was fine, she didn't need anyone, and she'd gotten this far on her own. It must be nice to have a family behind you along the way, though.

The galloping guitar intro of Barracuda suddenly blasting from her phone broke her out of her maudlin trance and back into the room.

Reaching over the side of the bed, she felt the sharp sting of a slap on her arse, *she couldn't really blame him for taking the opportunity when presented,* and with a tut, grabbed her iPhone.

Francine was calling.

AARON WOKE IN THE DARKNESS, A DULL ACHE PULSING IN HIS bladder. A few beers with Sophie while watching Creepshow had seemed like a great way to relax after their day's outing, but he had well and truly broken the seal and it was steadily working its way through him.

Sophie was delicately snoring away beside him, apparently unperturbed by the havoc the booze should be causing to her waterworks. He considered grabbing his phone and snapping a less than graceful photo of her while she was catching flies but thought better of it.

Stepping carefully out of bed the dizziness of the alcohol hit him, and he felt a little uneasy on his feet. Tactically weaving through the array of clothes and debris on the bedroom floor he made his was across the room.

As he passed the dolls on the coffin shaped bookcases, he failed to see their little plastic heads rotate in sync, the large creepy eyes following him as he moved.

Head down, arm pressed against the bathroom wall, Aaron watched the stream of piss dance about the toilet bowl, the stuttering stop-start of the flow of urine leaving him as relief filled his body.

He heard the vibrating buzz of a phone from the bedroom.

Who's calling in the middle of the night? He shook himself off before making his was back across the landing.

"Francine? What's up?" Sophies groggy voice answered as she accepted the call.

Aaron's silhouette filled the doorway, and he mouthed his confusion as Sophie looked up.

"Wait, Dora slow down. Take a breath, what's happened?"

The obvious note of alarm in her voice sobered Aaron as he stepped further into the room. "What's going on?"

Sophie's palm came up, shushing him as she listened to Dora on the other end of the call.

"Don't do anything. Make sure you're safe somewhere and wait for Grace to arrive…" Sophie's eyes widened, as she locked her gaze on the still confused Aaron. "Call the others and hold tight, we'll be right over, too."

"What the fuck is happening?" Aaron asked again, panic building inside him.

Taking advantage of the fresh confusion in the room, the dolls on the bookcases sprung to life and dove from their shelves down onto Aaron in a flurry of plastic mayhem.

"Fuck!"

Still slightly unsteady on his feet, Aaron toppled to the ground as the wall of plastic bodies hit him, their now lifelike limbs flailing and clawing at his naked form.

"Aaron!" Sophie yelped as she saw the attack happening. "Dora, just hold tight." She ended the call and scrambled across the room as dozens of twelve-inch dolls kicked and clawed at her boyfriend.

Aaron cast his arms out, sending dolls flying across the room as he fought to right himself and break free from the attack.

Dolls hung off his naked flesh in tight plastic grips, their fingers sinking in as they climbed all over him. Small sinister faces grinned and scowled as they swarmed his body.

Though small, their grips were like painful pinches all over his body, each with enough force to break skin, and Aaron winced as he struggled upright and began grabbing at the wriggling bodies before ripping them from his flesh. Each little demonic puppet felt like ripping a wax strip off his skin and the small streaks of blood left in their wake were beginning to add up.

Sophie dropped to her knees in front of Aaron and joined in, grabbing dolls two at a time and casting them as hard as she could against the wall. The panic spread across her face as she watched them stand back up like stuttering stop-motion nightmares and make their way back towards the fray.

Realising this was the case, Aaron began lifting the figures up and ripping their limbs away before casting them aside as Sophie followed suit.

The unrelenting assault continued, and the figurines clawed and scratched at them both as the pair began systematically dismantling them.

In just a few minutes they had managed to pull apart all the dolls and sat on the ground taking deep breaths as a room full of limbs and bodies still wriggled on the ground. Small doll heads, blinked and snarled up at them.

Aaron was covered in a series of cuts and grazes that bled weakly, but still left him looking like he'd received tickets to a trip through the paper cut factory and Sophie had received an array of cuts on her arms too.

"Get dressed," he said after taking in the full scale of madness across the room. "We need to get out of here, and we need to do it, like, now."

CHAPTER 12

Distant thunder rumbled as Chris stepped out of the car and gently closed the door behind him, painfully aware that it was barely six am and he didn't want to be the cause of breaking any local residents from their slumber.

He leaned backed on the car as his mind still reeled from his recent call with Dora.

The whole drive over, he'd gone over the call again and again in his head. Francine was dead. Murdered if what he had been told was correct.

A massive part of him suspected this to be some sort of distasteful prank. He wasn't oblivious to the slew of jokes at his expense from the group, and while it all felt pretty light-hearted, he had to wonder if maybe he really was the butt of the joke for them more often than he thought.

The alternative of course being that what Dora had told him was true. In which case, as awful as that was, did he really want to be caught up in whatever the ensuing situation would bring?

He continued to lean on the car as he took in the murky storm clouds in the distance doing their best to mask the arrival of the morning sun.

He could leave.

They didn't know he'd arrived yet, and he could just jump back in his car and head home again, nobody would be any the wiser. It really wasn't anything to do with him. Okay, so he did really like Francine – of all the Urb-Oboros collective, she'd been the one that seemed to speak to him with the most respect, but did that really put him on the same page as someone you would call when they turn up dead?

A wave of self-loathing washed over him as he was repulsed by his own spineless, self-serving mindset. Always the outlier when it came to making friends and here he was, debating running away when said friends needed him.

Finding the resolve he knew he had, he steeled himself and headed across the street and up the drive to Francine's home. He could be counted on to be there. He would be a solid, reliable friend.

Three swift raps and twenty seconds later, the door opened, and Chris was greeted by the grim face of Jack, his countenance bearing signs of panic, anger, and exhaustion.

"Chris, thanks for coming, you better come on in." Jack's eyes narrowed as he stepped to the side making room for Chris, while staring past his shoulder, out into the gloom of the street.

He stepped into the hallway and was hit by the familiar, stagnant pondwater smell he had been surrounded by earlier in the day. He could hear pacing coming from upstairs and a low, exhausted sob from the room to his left.

"Where…" his mouth felt drained of moisture, and he stumbled over his own tongue. "Should I go?"

"Head into the front room," Jack said with a nod in that direction.

He glanced briefly up the stairs, hearing footsteps and muttering as he passed into the room, and saw Dora on the sofa, knees hugged into her chest as she wept quietly.

Sophie was sat to her right, leaning in and stroking her hair delicately in a maternal manner that made Chris's stomach churn in a brief moment of mournful longing. Grace was kneeling on the floor before her, her hand softly caressing Dora's ankle in what Chris assumed to be her attempt at comforting her.

"Hi," he said sheepishly as three pairs of eyes fell on him. "I got here as soon as I could. What the hell is going on?"

"What's going on …" Jack said as he entered the room behind him. "Is some sick fuck has killed Francine, and we don't know who, or if this was a targeted thing or some random act of violence."

Dora's choking sobs grew louder at this, and Grace stood up, her face a portrait of rage. "I know I'm not the only one who can smell that swamp stink throughout the house. The same stink we all spent today bathed in, and I don't think the timing of this feels even remotely coincidental. We'd be a bunch of absolute idiots to sit around with our thumbs up our arses waiting for whoever the fuck this was to strike again."

"Wait, you mean that someone is after us as a group?" Chris's head swivelled left and right between Grace and Jack like a wind-up toy as panic set in further.

"I think you'd better take a look. Come on." Jack beckoned as he left the room.

Chris followed behind, panic already intensifying, with Grace taking up the rear as they headed into the kitchen, the damp stench in the air adding a metallic twang that caught in the back of his throat as they drew closer.

Jack sidestepped as he entered the room, allowing Chris a clear view into the kitchen, the scene unfolding before him as the new dawn cast a theatrical spotlight through the kitchen window.

Slumped on the white tile floor lay the body of Francine, her once olive skin now a dismal grey. Wicked shards of bone jutted from the pierced flesh at the top of both forearms, yellowed flaps of skin seemingly peeled back from the deep red tissue underneath.

She lay in a pool of pink water and where someone had lifted her tank top, Chris could see a fist sized hole in the centre of her stomach, the skin ruptured outwards like her insides had literally burst open. A mess of crimson and deep purple viscera bulged from the opening and what blood remained had dried to a dark, tar-like syrup.

"Oh God," Chris managed before his stomach lifted and he doubled over as he emptied the contents of his stomach onto the floor.

"That's about the size of it," Jack said as he leaned back against the wall. "In case you can't figure it out, it looks like she burst open with the force of what I could only imagine a fireman's hose would feel like."

"Except that's definitely the smell we're being assaulted with," Grace joined in. "It's from the cave. Or something like it."

Chris grabbed an old tea-towel that was resting on the radiator and wiped at his chin, the acrid taste lingering in his mouth and burning his nostrils. He wanted nothing more than a glass of water to swill the foulness away, but there was no chance he was stepping over Francine's body to reach the sink.

Jack opened the fridge and retrieved a diet Coke, passing it to Chris, clearly sensing his need. "Here, this'll have to do you."

Chris cracked the can and took a couple of long gulps before swilling it around to remove the taste from his mouth. "This is actually unreal. Part of me really thought this was some kind of sick joke."

"If only," Grace said as she headed back to the front room.

Jack stepped close to Chris and resting a hand on his shoulder, turned him from the room and motioned to follow Grace. "I'm sorry you needed to see that; I just think it's best to take in the severity of what's going on. Come on, let's get back to the others. I think we have a lot to discuss."

Back in the other room, Chris took a seat on the far end of the sofa as Jack continued to pace up and down. The tension could be cut with a knife and Dora's weak sobbing was like a dagger to the chest as everyone struggled with finding the right thing to say.

"Dora?" Sophie's voice broke the silence. "I know this is hard, but can you tell us what exactly happened, or I mean, as much as you can?"

She rubbed her sleeve under her nose and across her eyes as she sniffed softly, the sticky residue coating her arm glistening as she tried to compose herself.

"We …were talking on the phone. She was telling me about your trip and all the freaky stuff in the cave, and then she said she saw something in the garden and would call me back."

"And that was the last time you spoke to her?" Grace interjected.

"It was. I waited a little while and then got worried, like, who would be in her garden in the pouring rain, you know? I kept calling and calling when she didn't get back to me, but it just kept ringing out." Dora's eyes were glassy, and she was starting to tear up again. "I should have headed straight here as soon as she didn't pick up."

"And you still probably wouldn't have made it in time," Jack said. "That, or we'd have two bodies on our hands right now."

"Maybe so," she sniffed.

Sophie leaned forward and wiped at Dora's eyes with a balled-up tissue. "Is there anything else she said? Anything you can think of that might be any sort of clue?"

"She did say she was looking into the cave. She found some stuff on her laptop about a guy in prison. I don't see how that would be any help, though."

"It can't hurt to take a look at what she found, I suppose," said Chris.

A steady gallop of footsteps bounded down the stairs shortly before Aaron walked into the room, a face of thunder and irritation. It looked to Chris like he'd been dragged through a series of thorn bushes. His face and arms were a mess of cuts and grazes in tidy rows, almost like he'd been attacked with a fork.

"I still can't get hold of Rich," he said as he surveyed the room.

"What? I just assumed he wasn't here yet?" Chris said as the stakes seemed to have been immediately raised in his head, visions of Rich laid out somewhere in the same terrifying manner as Francine running through his mind.

"Nope, he's not picking up and given the circumstances, I'm a little bit worried," Aaron said as a bottle of beer seemed to appear from nowhere and he chugged on it. "To put it mildly."

On cue, a harsh wind rattled the windows in their frames, a whistling pitch running in tandem with the blast.

"We need to get over there. He's probably asleep, but I wouldn't want to chance sitting on it," Jack said, his eyes fixed on the window behind them.

"I agree," Sophie said. "All of us. Dora, you're coming too."

"shouldn't I call the police first? And stay here?"

"Fuck that," Grace said as she rose from the floor. "One emergency at a time, and you're not hanging around here on your own. We can call them as soon as we make sure Rich is okay."

"Absolutely. If you don't know where you're going, follow my car. Now, let's make like a tree and fuck off."

"Any weird shit on the way, you put your foot down, got it?" Jack said as he scooped up the laptop on the coffee table. "I'm taking this, too."

"Weird shit, what kind of weird shit?" Chris asked, his heartrate skyrocketing as they all began to move.

"You'll know. Come on." Aaron said patting him on the shoulder and making for the door.

CHAPTER 13

Rich was in a coffin.

This was a conclusion he'd come to very quickly when he had opened his eyes and found only darkness. The horizontal axis and his shoulders touching the sides of whatever container he was trapped in only strengthened that logic.

The initial thoughts of panic were offset by confusion, and he found himself taking a measure of his situation, shuffling his feet and quickly making contact with the rest of the box. His arms came up about a foot before hitting the rough wooden lid of his prison as he rotated his palms up and began to push at the lid with all his strength.

Finding absolutely zero give on the wood, panic finally joined the party as he began erratically slamming his fists at the lid screaming for help.

The sense of irony wasn't lost on him.

After winning a life changing amount of money, he'd instantly cut himself off from a huge amount of daily life, locking himself away from the public like a deranged maniac and closing his circle off to the world.

He bet people thought he was at the pissing in jars stage of his reclusion.

Finding himself in a literal box had closed that bubble even tighter, and perhaps there was some karmic humour to his fate. Somebody was making a point.

As he thrashed inside the box, he began to hear a solid thumping from above, as if in response to his hammering.

A triplet thud-thud-thud, echoed in his ears as he imagined nails being hammered into place, sealing his fate.

He woke up with a gasp, sitting bolt upright in his bed as he broke free from the dream, sweat soaked and panicking as his heart thumped in his chest like a jackhammer.

Thud-thud-thud.

His eyes darted about the room as he jerked his neck, trying to locate the source of the still hammering sound, before realising it was coming from the front door.

After jumping out of bed, he stepped into the sweatpants that lay on the ground and swept his dressing gown up from the banister as he passed, making his way down the stairs.

The door came open to an assembly of worried looking faces, huddled together with Aaron at the centre, his fist still raised ready to hit the door again.

"What, are you fucking deaf, Rich?" he said as he rudely pushed past him into the hall.

Rich stepped back and gestured with his arm to invite the rest of the group in. "I was asleep. Mind telling me why you're all here waking the dead?"

"The dead is exactly why we're here," Aaron said as he stepped back from the kitchen and poked his head into the front room. "Have you had any weird shit going on?"

"Other than at this very moment, you mean?" he responded, eyes wide at Aaron's bizarre bloodhound rendition. "Sophie, can you give me some sense here? Has he taken something? What sort of breakdown am I bearing witness to right now?"

He noticed for the first time, that Sophie's eyes were bloodshot, and she had a series of grazes on her face. Taking a moment to look at the rest of the group, he could see that Dora too had been crying and the obvious tension in the group hung heavy in the air.

"Francine's dead, Rich," Sophie said matter-of-factly.

"What?" Rich felt the colour drain from his face and the room span. "Can we go sit down? Come on in."

He led them into the front room and stepped back towards the fireplace, casting an arm across the room. "Excuse the mess but take a seat, I guess."

The group filed in and took their seats across the two large sofa's and began to fill Rich in on the situation with Francine, and how they'd reached this point in their journey. It was clear that each of them was unsettled by recent events, and the unknowing confusion, panic, and in at least one instance, the trauma, was hanging heavily over them.

Rich sat on the floor and calmly listened to Sophie and Grace as they took the lead with things, trying not to interrupt the tale but grimacing occasionally at the more disturbing parts of the story.

"And that brings us to here?" he asked as they reached their conclusion. "I'm really sorry I didn't get your calls, but I'm incredibly grateful that you all rushed to my aid."

"You've had no strange things happen, though? Jack asked.

"No, I pretty much came home, ate, and went to bed. Strange things like what?" Rich responded.

"I'd like to know about that too," Chris interjected. "You keep talking about weird things, and I feel like I'm totally in the dark here."

"Well, apart from what happened to Francine obviously, I got attacked by all of Sophie's dolls," Aaron said. "Hence why we both look like this."

"Hold up, dolls?" Rich's eyebrows met in the middle.

"Dolls. Exactly. Soph has a whole collection of living dead dolls and stuff, and they came to life and leapt off their shelves and tried to turn me into mincemeat."

"It's true," Sophie chimed in. "it was terrifying, we had to rip all their arms and legs off. And they kept moving."

"What the actual fuck?" Rich could feel the dizziness working itself back into his head.

"And I saw something in the reflection of my TV. I didn't think much of it at the time, but with all this, it feels like maybe I'm not going mad."

"Or we all are," said Sophie.

"Okay," Rich said, "Let's say this is really happening, has anyone else seen anything? Chris, Grace?"

"Nothing." Chris said, though his eyes were like dinner plates, and he looked more washed out than everyone else.

"Same, I haven't had anything happen either. I spent my evening with my…" she paused, "erm, *friend*, Moth. I headed straight over to Francine's when Dora called me.

A slight grin formed on Aaron's face. "Wait, back up. You've got a friend called Moth?"

Grace rolled her eyes. "It's Timothy, but that's not avant-garde enough apparently."

"Sounds like a tit." Aaron shot back.

Grace Flipped him off.

"So, we've got one very dead friend, another attack of inanimate objects and whatever the hell I saw. As fucked up as this all sounds, it still all points to us as a group being targeted." Jack was doing his best to remain as calm and focussed as he could, given the situation.

"And you still think its linked to the cave?" Chris asked.

"It seems too much of a coincidence not to be," Grace said. "That, and the smell of the water at Francine's was way too similar."

"Okay, okay, let's assume that all of this is actually real," Rich said as his fingers circled over his right eyelid, removing sleep, and emitting a satisfying squelch that only he could hear.

"You wouldn't be saying that if you'd just had a twelve-inch gothic bride digging its claws into your cock," Aaron said in response.

"I'm sure I wouldn't. And look, that's not my point here. What I'm saying is, if this is real and all signs point to it being so… where do we go from here?"

Everyone looked around the room at each other and it was obvious that nobody really had any answers. Dora and Sophie both looked about done with the situation, Aaron, Grace, and Jack looked ready to kick someone's teeth in and Chris looked like he could shit his pants at any moment. Rich still felt on the outskirts of the horror, and the weight of it hadn't really settled in yet.

After a short pause Rich broke the awkward silence. "Well, look, the questions we have right now are who and why? I suppose by the sounds of it, how is also a fair question."

"It's clearly something to do with the cave," Grace said. "Who or why isn't exactly clear, though. We didn't see anyone, and I don't know what we did to piss them off."

"Can we also not overlook the obvious, we were attacked by fucking dolls," Aaron added.

"Yeah, this isn't just a case of some*one* we've pissed off," Sophie said, rubbing the much-used ball of tissue under her nose, the skin already beginning to look raw. "It's some thing."

Jack brushed a few old Coke cans along the coffee table, placed Francine's laptop down and opened it. The screen's glow filled the room.

"Maybe whatever Francine found on here can shed some light. I'm not hopeful, but we can see."

Dora and Sophie both moved from their places and sat down on the floor either side of Jack as he began to scroll through the still open page.

Three sets of eyes darted over the document as Jack scrolled, pausing occasionally to mutter a single "Done?" before carrying on. The silence was broken by the odd gasps or looks of confusion and wide-eyed shock as they took in what they were reading.

"I can see how this would seem like nonsense before everything kicked off," Jack said as he paused at a particularly confusing part of the page. "But given what we have going on here now, it seems like there could be a link."

"For sure. He walks into a bank and blows a hole in the roof and then he just sits down and waits for the police to turn up, that's not normal behaviour." Sophie chewed on the end of a pen she'd picked up from the coffee table.

"And then they pin the deaths of his friends on him with seemingly no evidence," Dora chimed in as she re-read the last part of the page.

"Zero history with the law and then kills all his friends and walks into a bank to intentionally get caught. It definitely doesn't add up," Jack agreed.

"Plus, look at this," she pointed to a section on the screen. "Says here that he'd been in prison less than a week before he broke a man's neck in a scuffle."

Rich spluttered abruptly. "I think you and I have a very different definition of the word scuffle."

"Whatever," she waved away his comment. "He broke his neck and kept screaming '*It was her*' over and over as they dragged him away. Something seriously fucked up is going on here, guys."

A huge crack of thunder rolled outside, seemingly punctuating Dora's statement and everyone jumped as a bright burst of lightning flooded the room with light a few seconds later.

"Whatever this is, or was, it sounds like he thought he could lock himself away from it," Jack said.

"And now whatever it is, it's after us. Fantastic." Rich stood up from the couch and wrapped his dressing gown more tightly around himself, realising he was completely underdressed for dealing with this,

"This guy might have more information on what exactly it is we're dealing with," Grace added. "It's a lead, I suppose."

"The only one we have right now. Something to go off, anyway." Sophie stood up from the floor and moved to the window, tentatively fingering the blinds apart to look outside.

The morning was well under way now, but with the hammering rain lashing down from the storm clouds above, it appeared much earlier than it was. The Cul-de-sac was still deadly quiet, and the only sound outside was the rainfall battering against the cars and plastic bins out on the street.

"Guys…" Aaron's voice came from somewhere at the back of the house. "You might want to come see this."

They all jumped up and rushed from the room, following the sound of his voice until they found him stood in the middle of the large glass conservatory.

Lightning had struck the ground at the far end of the garden, sending up the earth below in a spray of mud and grass.

Rich felt his bowels loosening, his stomach seeming to churn in time with his racing heart.

Barely seconds later, it struck again, a little closer this time, and for the briefest of moments there appeared be the form of a tall, angular woman with flowing white hair and blue-grey skin stood in its wake, a thin silken robe seeming to cling to her torso like water flowing down stream.

The figure was gone as soon as it arrived, and the group shared silent, questioning glances with each other before the lightning struck again a few second later.

Again, it was just a little closer than before, and this time the figure appeared like a withered, emaciated crone. Her wet hair clung to her body and the leathery flesh looked gently placed onto its skeletal frame, a cruel mouth of crooked yellow teeth met them as their blood ran cold.

"Guys..." Chris stuttered. "You're all seeing this right?"

"Yes." Jack clenched his fists as his whole body tensed.

The lightning struck again as more earth flew up around it and steam rose from the small crater on the ground.

The white-haired woman had returned, but this time didn't disappear. Her cold black eyes stared into their souls as they watched her lips begin to part.

They watched on, the wind and rain whipping around her as she raised a delicate arm up towards them, droplets of rainwater shimmering against her smooth, cool skin, and beckoned to them seductively with a finger, the talon-like fingernail curving back and forth as she invited them closer.

Her smile widened uncomfortably as it began to stretch beyond human proportions and they winced in unison as the edges of her plump, pink lips started to split at the seams, the skin tearing along her cheeks and up towards her jaw. The twin lacerations of flesh began to open up revealing the deep red tissue beneath and her mouth opened unnaturally wide to show rows of sharp teeth, bright against her pink gums.

An ear-splitting shriek pierced the air as she screamed sending a physical shockwave out towards them as the glass windows of the conservatory shattered, showering them in a rain of broken glass.

Aaron fell backwards through the doorway into the huddled group, toppling them like bowling pins as he landed in a heap atop them.

"Fuck this!" he bellowed as he jumped back up, registering the fresh pain from the shards of glass embedded in his skin. "Everyone run. Now!"

They scrambled to right themselves, tumbling and groping at each other as they struggled to escape the pile of bodies and broken glass that they'd become, before immediately rushing for the front door.

Grace threw herself on the door and swung it open as the wind blasted a spray of rain into her face. Stepping back, she allowed Sophie, Dora, and Chris to charge past her before she followed suit with Jack and Rich and Aaron taking up the rear.

Out in the storm they ran to the cars, Aaron and Sophie jumping into the front of the Ford with Dora and Rich diving into the back. Jack threw open the back door of the Audi and yelled for Grace and Chris to get in before dashing around the other side to hop into the driver's seat and fire up the engine.

"Where are we going?" he called from the window as Aaron reversed at speed, coming parallel with him.

"It doesn't fucking matter, just drive."

CHAPTER 14

The citrus smell of disinfectant was heavy in the air and carried a bizarre freshness that contrasted with the damp stink of their sodden forms as they sat waiting in the hotel lobby.

Grace and Jack sat on an uncomfortable, powder blue sofa across from Chris and Dora, seated on an identical sofa of an awful pink variety. The rain-soaked foursome did their best to look inconspicuous as they waited for Rich to return.

Stood outside the huge wall of glass that served as the buildings entrance, Aaron and Sophie waited just in eye-line of the group, ready for the nod to come inside when rooms were sorted.

It had been decided swiftly in the hotels carpark that walking in with one of them dripping blood and a pattern of glass shards sticking from their body wouldn't exactly expediate their ability to source some rooms, and so they'd agreed to wait outside on high alert.

The drive from Rich's house had been a breakneck mini convoy of adrenaline and panic, and it was Rich who had decided to steer them in the direction of the nearest Travelodge. His logic being that while they needed somewhere to hole up, a place filled with other people seemed like the most sensible of choices. A decision that nobody else in the car could find fault with, and the rest of the group in Jacks car had clearly put two and two together as they tailed behind Aaron to their destination.

They sat waiting for Rich's return, lost in thought, each of them recounting the recent scene of unexplainable terror in their heads.

Dora had returned to an almost catatonic state as she seemed to curl in on herself like a lost child, Chris had the complexion of a sickly Victorian widow that wouldn't see out winter, and Jack, much like Grace herself, looked ready to go to war.

"Your rooms are ready." Rich appeared back at the waiting group; three keycards fanned in his fingers.

"Any issues?" Jack asked as he stood and gave the nod to Sophie waiting outside the building.

"Compared to the last hour, a walk in the park."

Aaron and Sophie walked through the automatic doors as the squawk of a bell sounded, swiftly making their way over to the group. Aaron was looking positively awful, and Jack winced as he glanced at the numerous pieces of glass that were still jutting from his arms.

"We're good?" he asked, his face a grimace of pain.

"Yeah, rooms are sorted, let's head up," Rich said as he started to walk away.

They all followed behind him, naturally forming a human shield to block the receptionists view of Aaron as they moved.

"I didn't think anyone would want their own room," Rich continued, "So I got a room for Aaron and Sophie, one for Dora and Grace and I figured the guys would share."

"Won't it be best if you we all stay together?" Chris asked.

"Yeah, probably while were awake for sure, but I didn't want to assume on sleeping arrangements and it would ring a lot more alarm bells if we booked one room and tried to cram us all in."

Grace was impressed. "Have you done this before?"

"Booked hotel rooms, yes. Been on the run from some sort of…" he paused.

"Demon witch?" Grace confirmed.

"Yeah…not so much."

"Same." Dora mumbled as she walked alongside them, her arms wrapped tightly around herself.

"I made sure all the rooms are on the same floor too, and two of them are connected if we want to unlock both sides of the adjoining doors."

They reached the elevators and Rich tapped the button as they waited in silence for the lift to arrive.

"Aargh, fuck," Aaron yelped as Sophie extracted another piece of glass from his arm.

Blood seeped from the wound before she had time to press a padded square of gauze firmly over the cut, applying as much pressure as she could.

Rich winced at the sight, pitying his friend, but also guiltily felt relieved that the shower of exploding glass from the conservatory windows hadn't really got him.

To the side of the bed where Aaron lay, was a makeshift operating table.

Jack and Grace had volunteered to go out into the city and source what they could to help patch him up, much to Aaron's objections.

Gauze, plasters, bandages, alcohol, and antiseptic made up the bulk of the supplies, though Jack had also insisted on superglue – which he assured everyone was one of the best things to seal small cuts and had been used in wars to seal soldier's injuries.

"Don't be such a baby," Jack said. "Your girlfriend is doing an incredible job of playing nurse here."

"That's easy for you to say, you're not the one covered head to toe in frigging cuts."

He ran a couple of fingers over the rough line on his cheek that he'd taken his own advice on and superglued earlier. "No, just a couple of small nicks, I guess. You'll be fine once she's got you bandaged up, though."

"Until she turns up again," Dora said flatly from her seat in the corner of the room.

"I think we'll be safe for now, though I know I can't guarantee that." Rich sat on the side of the bed, next to Aaron, looking out the window at the view of the city. The storm looked to have disappeared for now and the sun was high in the sky leaving a view that looked bright and promising and a vast contrast to the hellscape they had just fled from.

Chris stirred from his place sat on the ground, his back leaning on the wall. "We still need to figure out where we go from here. We can't stay locked in this hotel room forever and whatever she is, she's probably going to keep coming for us." His voice cracked a little, betraying his obvious nerves. "We either need to find out who she is and how to stop her or figure out what we did wrong and see if we can undo it. I'm not too proud to admit I'm terrified here, and it does feel like we're living out some sort of horror movie situation."

"That means at least one of us will survive then. Wonderful," Sophie said as she continued to patch up Aaron.

"For you maybe," Rich added. "They're called final girls, not final guys."

The electronic click of the doors locking mechanism sounded, and everyone tensed, focus turning to the door as Grace stepped in and they immediately relaxed again.

"Okay, so some good news," she said. "I worked all the magic I could muster, and I've secured us a prison visit tomorrow with Johnson."

How did you manage that?" Jack asked.

"Told them I worked for Netflix and we're doing some preliminary research for a new documentary series. They said they can't promise he will actually agree to the visit, but I said to tell him that we know about the cave. Hopefully that will be enough to pique his interest."

She crossed the room and took a seat on the edge of the bed, wincing at the sight of Aaron's injuries and the array of bloody gauze that had accumulated on their workstation.

Rich was seriously impressed. Booking a few hotel rooms was one thing, but Grace had just secured entry to a high security prison off the back of a phone call.

"Hopefully he'll see fit to turn up and maybe give us some answers," Rich said as he scanned the carpark from his vantage point at the window. "Assuming that is, that he isn't just crazy. Which is a distinct possibility."

Jack tilted his head, emitting a satisfying crack from his neck which caused a look of disgust from Grace. "For the time being, lets run with the idea that he's not. It doesn't seem too likely that he's going to have a solution for us, or he probably wouldn't be in a cell right now, but any information he can give us at all is going to be a massive help."

"Anything we can do to fight it is going to put us in a better stead than we're in right now though, right?" Sophie added as she finished putting the last of the dressings on Aaron's injuries.

Aaron shimmied up the bed into a slouch and kissed Sophie on the forehead. "If he's in the same boat as us, he's managed to survive for what, thirty years? That's going to account for something."

"I guess we'll find out tomorrow. Now what do we do until then?" Rich turned and rested his palms on the windowsill as he glanced around their adequate, yet cramped accommodation.

Aaron was beginning to resemble a modern patchwork Frankenstein creation, though he seemed to be taking it all in his stride, which considering he was the only one to really be injured so far, said a lot.

Dora was still sat in her seat, shrinking inside herself, withdrawn to a worrying state of near catatonia that she only broke for the occasional monosyllabic additions to the conversation.

"I can't speak for everyone." Aaron winced as he sat upright on the bed, "But I'm not leaving this hotel until we head to this prison tomorrow."

"Agreed," Sophie added immediately.

"No arguments here," Jack also agreed.

"We should be safe here I would hope, but it still might be a good idea to sleep in shifts." Rich wondered if he was taking too much of a leadership role here and left it at that.

"S-m-r-t," said Aaron with a grin.

"We can just open up these two rooms and stay here. Fuck the other room." Rich shuffled past the bed and across the room, unlocking and opening the door that connected through to the next bedroom.

As if in response to their plans, the telephone on the desk sprang to life, shocking everyone into silence as they stared at the blinking green light on the display as it rang, panic-stricken faces looking at the phone like it was completely alien to them.

Rich already upright, moved to the desk and tentatively reached for the receiver, his stomach lurching.

"Wait," Chris snapped, the colour drained from his face. "Just ignore it."

"It could just be the front desk," Rich said as he lifted the earpiece.

Static filled his ear for a second before he pressed the button on the phone putting it on loudspeaker.

The line continued to crackle with static for a few seconds before the voice began. "You…" the female voice sounded deep and sultry, while carrying an obvious air of malice. "…entered this world kicking and screaming from the waters of the womb, how fitting it is that you shall leave it the same way."

Rich felt a wave of dizziness hit him again and felt unsteady on his feet. This was his first actual instance of firsthand dealing with whatever this was, and the fear felt far more real that it had previously.

"What is it you want?" he asked, a noticeable quiver in his voice, though he was trying his best to keep his cool.

The breathy wheezing on the end of the line continued for a couple of seconds, sounding thick with mucous as it filled the room before the voice continued, "Five more sacrificial lambs await the slaughter, and I am coming for you."

The line went dead, the dial tone buzzing loudly as they all stared, wide-eyed about the room at each other.

Rich placed the receiver down and stumbled backwards, taking a seat near the foot of the bed next to Grace; his pulse was pounding at his temples and his mouth felt drained of all moisture.

His tongue roamed his teeth, trying to bring some much-needed saliva back into his mouth as he sniffed. "She knows where we are, then."

CHAPTER 15

With a slow and steady creep that wouldn't look out of place in any archaic black and white villain movie, Chris tiptoed quietly towards the door.

The purring sound of Dora's gentle snoring carried across the room as he glanced to the bed she and Grace slept on, spooning peacefully into each other. Jack lay on the pull-out mattress below, curled up in the foetal position to accommodate himself on a bed obviously sized for a child.

He paused for a moment, mentally battling with himself over his decision before he carefully turned the handle of the door and slipped out into the hallway.

Five more sacrificial lambs await the slaughter.

Hours had passed since the phone call and the group had for the most part, managed to calm themselves and made plans for the next day as well as heading down to the hotel restaurant for dinner, a task that in itself seemed terrifying as they spent every second on a cautious high alert.

The entire time, Chris had the same two words repeating over and over in his head, the wheezy phlegm filled rasp a soundtrack of growing unease.

Five more.

It seemed to have gone unnoticed to everyone else in the room, but not to Chris.

There were seven of them.

He ran through all the possibilities he could think of in his mind, and the frontrunner as far as theories went, was the one he'd originally thought of.

This was nothing to do with him.

This was some other issue that the group had found themselves in and had nothing to do with the cave.

It made sense.

He was well aware of the rest of the group being more bonded in friendship with each other than they were with him. They were all a similar age and shared far more in common than he did with any of them. This had to be some other event that he wasn't party to that had come back to bite them in the arse.

The other possibility was that whatever this was, it did affect them all, but for some reason there was an allotted fatal quota in place, and while that was a frightening concept, it was really every man for himself.

He cast a final glance back over his shoulder at the door to their room before he pressed the chrome button to call up the lift.

"THE FUCKING COWARDLY SHITHOUSE TWAT!"

Aaron flipped the makeshift medical table, sending blood-soaked gauze and medical supplies across the room as his outburst intensified.

It was clear that he had taken Rich's bombshell about Chris's disappearance far worse than anyone else, and the rest of the group gave him the room to rage as Sophie tried to calm him down.

"Look, we don't know that he's done a runner. He might have left for something else," Rich tried saying from a safe distance.

"Bullshit. The piss ant has done one and we all know it."

"Seems likely," Jack added. He too was visibly seething at the betrayal.

"And the worst of it isn't even that he's ran off like a chickenshit," Aaron continued. "It's the fact he did it while we were all sleeping, completely helpless."

"Okay, it doesn't look great. But we're all okay so it's not worth opening up your cuts over." Rich found himself wondering why he was defending Chris, but it was more that he was finding the silver lining in the situation.

"He could have been taken," Grace offered as she removed a soiled piece of bloody fabric from the bedsheets between her finger and thumb and dropped it onto the floor beside her.

"Silently? Nah, we'd have heard something," said Jack.

Seeming to have finally run out of steam, Aaron moved to drop into the chair at the corner of the room, ending his tantrum.

"He either comes back or he doesn't, this doesn't change any of our original plans," Rich said. "It's my watch, so I suggest everyone try get back to sleep and get what rest you can. Jack, I'll give you a shake in a couple of hours, try not to attack me, yeah?"

"I'm not making any promises." He grinned.

Sophie crossed the room and gripped Aaron's hand. "Come on, give Rich the chair and let's try get back to sleep."

He stood up as he was led back into the other room, resting a hand on Rich's shoulder as he passed. "Shout if anything happens, especially if Chris comes back. I've got a few choice words to share with him."

"Will do."

Rich angled the chair towards the door and sat down with a sigh, the chair eliciting a groan of its own as he settled into it.

Was this really happening?

Were they really hiding out in a Travelodge on the run from some otherworldly demoness, resting up before journeying to visit a convicted criminal to ask for tips on how to stop her. Everything about this seemed so insane that he really couldn't fully get to grips with it.

Chris had been right about one thing – this did feel like some sort of horror movie situation. That thought didn't sit well with him at all, and he thought of the countless slasher movies he'd watched over the years. He couldn't think of a single one where the fat guy survived. A chilling thought really.

He pondered the situation as it was and wondered if there was perhaps an easier way out of this. How far reaching was her threat, could he just book them all on a flight to the Bahamas and lay low for a while sipping pina coladas on the beach?

But for how long?

He didn't imagine this would just blow over and was sure they'd spend the entire time waiting for something to come after them regardless. Money probably wasn't enough to buy them out of this and seeing it through with whatever their plan was, looked to be their only option.

He felt the weight of everything bearing down on him as he focused on staying vigilant, but as time passed, he could feel the lack of sleep setting in, and his eyelids started to feel heavy.

Caffeine.

He needed coffee if he was to remain focussed, and for the first time in his life, he thanked the higher powers for awful hotel room provisions.

Easing gently out of the chair, he stepped to the desk and lifted the small plastic kettle, its once pristine white now a tarnished yellow. The colouring reminded him of thick layers of dead skin, like the soles of the feet of women in the readers wife's section of old porno mags they found discarded under bridges as teens.

After filling the kettle as silently as possible in the bathroom sink, he returned it to its dock and flicked the switch, shaking out a sachet of coffee before tearing it open and depositing it into a mug as he waited for the water to boil.

The gurgling pop of water reaching boiling point was just beginning to make itself known when the electronic click of the lock sounded at the door to the room.

Startled by the sound, Rich's eyes darted about the room searching for anything he could use as a weapon, before immediately giving up and stepping empty handed towards the now opening door.

With a drawn-out squeak of hinges, the door slowly swung open to reveal Chris, a dour expression plastered across his pale face as he stepped into the room.

Rich's wide-eyed moment of panic started to pass, and he deflated as he stepped forward; Chris's lips now pursed, the creases of his brow doubling as he raised his eyebrows in a silent acknowledgement.

"Chris, what the hell, man? We thought you'd ran out on us," Rich said as he threw his hands up in the air dramatically.

"My apologies," he said as he stepped towards him.

The knife in his grip, appearing as if from nowhere, sunk into Rich's body just above the waist as Chris's expression transformed into a vengeful sneer.

CHAPTER 16

The woman lying in the hospital bed looked as close to death as one could put into visual perception. Her withered, emaciated form was equal parts wrinkled, greying flesh and various medical tubing.

Saline drips, feeding tubes and intravenous lines of medication ran from her body like a spiderweb of finality. This all paired with the oxygen mask and catheter made for a flesh puppet that was plugged from every angle.

Her hands had been bound in large white mittens to prevent her continual attempts to rip the tubes from her body. An obvious necessity, but Chris thought they looked like cotton boxing gloves.

Regardless, it prevented him from doing the one thing he wanted to do more than anything right now, which was hold her hand.

Sitting in the chair that he'd pulled to the side of the metallic scaffold-like structure that was her deathbed, he settled for just stroking her forearm repeatedly, an action that served just to let her know someone was there.

He had no idea if she was aware of his presence or not, and none of the hospital staff seemed to be able to answer that question either.

If she could though …

Chris's eyes stung as he sat in silence. He may have run out of tears for now, but he knew the burning sensation wouldn't be leaving him anytime soon, and the pink, glassy eyes that met his reflection anytime he had to visit the bathroom were a constant reminder of his misery.

The framework of medical apparatus that sandwiched her bed beeped in a continual pattern that he had by now managed to block out, and the green and blue electronic charts danced up and down as the readings on the end ticked up and down minutely as time passed.

With just over an hour before the nurse was due back to adjust her, Chris wallowed in lachrymose despair. This in turn added a level of guilt and shame into the cocktail of emotions.

His mother lay there as the lifeforce ebbed from her body and he was moping about how sad he felt. The irony that if he wasn't sad, what did that say about his love for her?

There really was no way to win against this influx of feelings and there certainly wasn't a handbook in dealing with grief and bereavement.

Everyone deals with things in their own way.

That felt like an absolute cop out as far as giving him something to focus on. Something to tell him that how he was feeling was correct.

Standing up, he was hit by the chemically, clinical stink of the room. He couldn't explain it, but it felt like the slightest movement disturbed the very air around him, bringing the previously unnoticed smell of sterility back to the forefront of his senses.

After lifting the plastic jug from the trolley beside him, he poured a measure of the weak orange drink into a cup and fished around in a bag for a fresh sponge swab. The pink foam-tipped stick resembled a lollipop, and he dipped it into the juice before bringing it to his mother's lips.

The act seemed entirely pointless, and it felt more like he was basting her lips than providing any source of hydration. He hated doing it, and felt both unskilled and lacking in providing the care she needed, but he didn't know what else to do.

Sit here and watch her die.

That was what it came down to. There was certainly no dignity in death, and he thought that when his time comes, he would gladly take a massive heart attack over this.

Giving up on the fruitless attempts at hydration, he sat back down again and clasped both hands tightly around her mittened hand.

"Mum," he managed as his throat constricted around his words, cracking his voice as he spoke. "I love you more than I could ever put into words."

A searing pain exploded across his face as he screamed. It felt like acid had been cast into his face, searing his flesh as the pain somehow felt both physical and mental.

CHAPTER 17

"**H**elp!"

Rich yelped as he managed to grapple Chris's wrist in both hands and fought with all his strength to keep the blade from sinking in any further.

The sharp tip of the kitchen knife was currently two inches deep into his stomach, to the right of his bellybutton and he wrestled with his attacker, trying to pull the blade from his flesh like the mythical sword in the stone before giving up and falling backwards onto the ground, removing himself from the attack, but leaving himself prone for another attempt.

Instantly up on his elbows, Rich tried to edge backwards, shuffling his feet on the carpet underneath him for momentum as the now malevolent face of Chris stared down at him.

The pain of the attack still hadn't registered, but he could feel the warm fluid leaking from his stomach as blood poured from the wound. *Thank God for dark colours.*

As he shimmied backwards like a dog dragging its arse across a carpet, he saw a shape move above him.

Dora stepped over him, and without hesitation, picked up the kettle from the desk and cast its boiling contents across the room into the face of their attacker.

Chris let out a blood-curdling scream as the boiling water hit the side of his face. He dropped the knife and clasped at his blistering skin.

A second later he was flung sideways like a ragdoll as Aaron barrelled into him through the open door that adjoined both rooms, sending them into a sprawling heap on the ground.

"Stop, please," came the panicked voice of Chris. "I need help, please stop it." His plea sounded desperate and came out more like a sob than a request.

Aaron was flailing wildly on top of him, swinging fists erratically as Chris clutched at his scorched face.

"She was controlling me," Chris wailed as he tried to shield himself from Aaron's raining blows.

Grace and Sophie appeared in a pincer formation and dragged them apart. Jack moved to Rich, who lay against the base of the bed, both palms pressed firmly over his knife wound.

Chris curled into a ball and wept as he clutched at his face, his sobs a sobering moment of reflection for everyone in the room.

CHRIS SAT AGAINST THE WALL; KNEES SKYWARD AS HE HELD the bag of ice to the side of his face, His sobs had died out, but the pain resonated from him, and his now good eye stared vacantly at the door to the room.

"Chris, I'm so sorry," Dora pleaded, her face wracked with the turmoil of recent events. "I just saw you with the knife over Rich and acted without thinking."

He pulled the bag of ice away from his burnt face as he turned to meet her gaze. Her horrified expression told him everything he needed to know.

The left side of his face glistened like a waxwork, the skin a red mess of fluid filled blisters. The skin around his eye was puffy and swollen shut and his eyebrow looked distorted and stretched thin, the hair patchy and missing in places. His left ear had swelled to an alarming size, a silvery sheen reflecting across its pink misshapen surface.

"It's okay," he said, waving his free hand dismissively. "I wasn't me, what else could you do?"

Jack cleared his throat from across the room. "He's right. At the time he was a threat and you reacted; you can't beat yourself up about it. If anything, we now know that if she takes control of someone, we can break it."

"I still feel terrible though, I mean Chris your face … that has to be so painful."

He pressed the icepack back to his cheek, wincing as it made contact with the scorched flesh. "It's agony, but you could have done worse and it's better this than me having killed you all. I feel sick thinking about it, being controlled like a puppet."

"it's good to know you didn't desert us either," Jack added.

Chris felt the shame burning within him and thought about how he had stepped out of the hotel lobby, ready to abandon them to their fate. The only upside to his ruined face was that shame wouldn't be obvious on his flushed face.

"Of course."

"How did it work?" Jack continued. "Were you like a passenger while she was in the driving seat? Watching but unable to do anything?"

Chris felt the bile rising in his throat and swallowed back vomit as he briefly relived those moments.

"No," he said, a seriousness taking over him. "It was like I was pushed into a dream. She made me relive the worst day of my life."

Dora knelt and rested her hand on his knee, cocking her head as she gave him a sympathetic smile. She seemed to have broken free from the shock that had enshrouded her, and Chris thought that was as least some sort of silver lining.

In the next room over, Rich lay on the bed, pleading his case.

"It's fine. Just a dressing will do, it doesn't even really hurt."

"you've been fucking stabbed, stop being a twat." Sophie brandished a tube of superglue in the air, wiggling it like a threat.

"You're not supergluing a knife wound."

"I thought you said it wasn't that bad?" Aaron grinned from the chair in the corner of the room.

"It's really not, but I still don't want you to squirt glue into it!" Rich said, acting like a child bargaining with a doctor over a jab.

"Look," Sophie said in as stern a voice as she could muster up. "We're doing it whether you like it or not. It was pissing blood, and we don't need it opening up more, especially if we have to run again. The choice is letting me do it or I get Aaron to sit on your chest while I do it."

"Kinky."

Shut the fuck up, Aaron!" both Rich and Sophie shot in tandem.

"Enough with the melodrama," Grace finally piped up from her place across the room, leaning against the bathroom door. "Rich, just let Sophie play nurse for two minutes and then we can get down to figuring out what our next move is."

"Nobody sleeps," came Jacks voice from the next room.

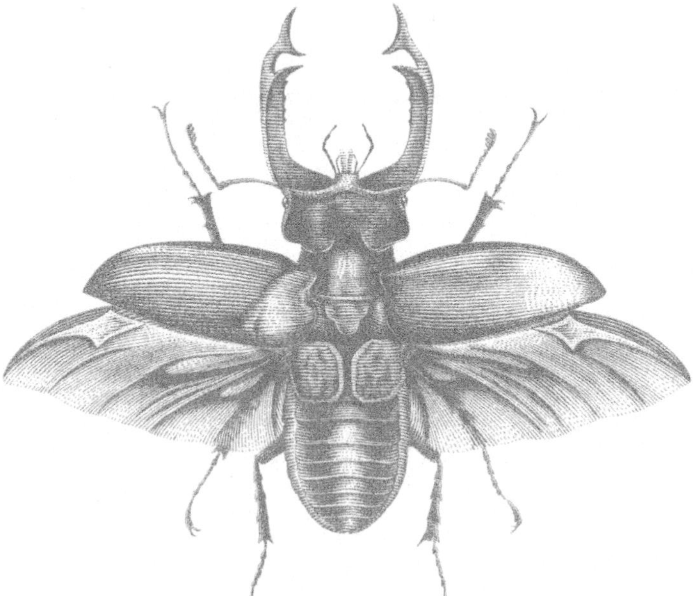

CHAPTER 18

What seemed more miraculous to the group than making it through the rest of the night unhindered, was managing to sneak Aaron and Chris out of the hotel without raising any alarms.

Thankfully, the maroon colouring of Rich's blood-soaked hoodie hid a multitude of sins to the uninterested.

Aaron's patchwork of cuts and Chris's now grotesque appearance were much more obvious, but somehow they managed to sneak out the hotel lobby and made it to the car park without detection.

"We're agreed then?" Rich asked. "Grace and I will go inside to see him, while you guys wait outside the prison."

"They're not going to let us all pile in to see him, and It would raise alarm bells if we tried," Jack agreed. "That, and I hardly think Chris and Aaron look like TV execs right now. No offense."

"I'm definitely offended," Aaron said as he pressed an open hand to his chest. "Yeah though, makes sense. Get in, pump the guy for info and get out. what could go wrong?"

"Don't invoke Murphy's law, dickhead." Rich shot Aaron a playful scowl.

"What?"

"Anything that can go wrong, will go wrong," Chris answered for him.

"Oh, okay. Sorry, we don't all watch Frasier."

Rich flipped him off as he climbed into the back of the car.

"Same rules as before," Jack said to Aaron. "See anything weird, get the hell out of there."

The journey took just over an hour, and Jack was struggling to stay awake.

The weather had taken a positive turn and returned to the blistering heat of summer, something that generally would be a welcomed warmth, but for Chris it must have been like pouring salt into the wound, so Jack kept the AC cranked right up so it was positively chilly in his

Audi. Chris lay down in the back to avoid as much direct sunlight as possible.

Grace appeared lost in thought and Jack gripped the wheel tightly and glanced in the mirror at the look of resolute focus cemented on his scowling face.

He was ready for anything this bitch could throw at him.

His determination to be prepared for whatever threat came next, and he had no doubt it was coming, was the driving force in remaining calm.

Calm and vigilant, that was how they got out of this mess.

The dense forest of trees that sandwiched the road was a blur of vibrant green as they whizzed past at sixty, deciding in advance that being pulled for speeding would do them no favours right now, and for a brief moment Jack's eye was caught by a break in the blur of luscious greens and browns.

She stood between two tall trees; her silken hair being carried by the wind in what would have made a beautiful image if not attached to the threatening wide smile of the blue-grey skinned hell witch that was hunting them. The shimmering, opalescent dress clung tightly to her curves in the breeze and her hand was raised to the sky, less a wave and more like the desperate signal of a hitchhiker.

Jack choked on his own saliva and gripped white-knuckle tight to the wheel as he sped up, closing the gap on Aaron's car. A full body shiver came with an involuntary neck twitch, and he shook it off before glancing back into the wing mirror.

Gone.

They soon arrived at the massive redbrick structure that was their destination, its high walls and monstrous blue metal door looming over them.

Jack pulled up behind Aaron and killed the engine. His heart still felt like it was beating out of his chest, but he mentally willed himself into an at least fake calm.

Grace was just readying herself to step out the car when a trio of alert noises sounded.

"What now?" she said, pulling her phone from her pocket as the others did likewise.

(13:34) **JustVictor:**
I do not think I can make it this time friends. So sorry.

(14:22) **Spooky_Sophie66:**
Oh Victor, that sucks. Much sadface.

(20:07) **Chris.Miller1975:**
Hi Folks, here are the photos from today's Cave expedition.

(20:08) **Chris.Miller1975:**
(Dropbox/Urb/July22)

(20:10) **Chris.Miller1975:**
Had a great time as we've come to expect. Looking forward to the next one!

(21:14) **Francine_Nightcrawler(Admin):**
Thanks Chris, be good to take a proper close look at them. Those carvings/gems around that hole are fascinating.

(22:22) **Dora.T.Explorer:**
>Oh wow! I missed out with this one. Those symbols are crazy, is that a snake fighting an eagle?

(22:38) **Spooky_Sophie66:**
>was cool. You were missed, lovely.

(11:04) **JustVictor:**
>Sorry to say I missed this explore. Looks like it was much fun. Pictures are good Chris. I have seen those symbols much in my grandmother's home.

Aaron and the others stepped from their car and made their way to Jack's Audi, phones in hand, concern on each of their faces.

"Guys, you've read this right? We need to get on the phone to Victor immediately." Sophie waved her phone wildly in the air.

Jack leaned against the side of the car and surveyed the area, partly to get a lay of the land and partly because he feared a return visit from the monochrome menace..

The car park was small and mostly empty, except for a row of about ten cars lined up on the other side of the entrance and a solitary, beat up old Fiesta a few spaces away from them. A middle-aged woman with short coppery hair sat in the passenger seat sobbing weakly.

No insidious creeping killers for now.

"One problem at a time," he said, realizing everyone had left Sophie's question unanswered.

"Don't you think they're sort of the same problem, though?" She shot Jack a look that was far sterner than he had ever seen her.

"Okay, you have a point, but we need to deal with the current hurdle first, right?" He knew that he was taking the lead with things, something that seemed to be coming extremely natural to him but didn't want to become bossy with it. Also, Sophie was one of the most genuinely positive people he had ever met.

Of all the goths in the world, he had ended up friends with a cheerful one. Trust him to find the defect.

"Fuck's sake, Jack, do you have to sit down to piss? Rich and Grace are going in to speak to this guy, do you want us to just sit around with our thumbs up our butts while we wait? What is it with men and the inability to multi-task!"

Jack shot Aaron a look and received an apathetic shrug for his troubles.

"Babe, I think Jack means we can't go running off to deal with another lead," Aaron interjected, trying for what was probably the first time in his life to deescalate things. "We can get Victor on the phone while we're waiting for Rich to get back and hopefully go from there. Cool?"

"That's what I meant. Christ, why is everything always so difficult?" Sophie pouted.

Grace chipped a large stone across the carpark with her boot, sending it skipping out into the road.

"Maybe because we're being hunted by a swamp hag. I agree with the plan, though, Rich and I will go see what this guy is about, assuming that he will turn up, and you guys can see what Victor can tell us about things for when we get back."

Jack sidled over to Aaron as the discussion continued, a sheepish look on his face as he weighed up whether to add to the group hysteria.

"Hey, on the drive over did you—"

"See the bitch from the cave? Yup."

Jack relaxed his shoulders and sighed. "Good. Well, not good, but I'm not seeing things at least."

"Sophie saw her too, I'm not sure about Rich and Grace. They didn't let on if they did, though."

"There's no getting away from this, is there?" Jack tried not to let the dread of the situation show on his face, but he didn't think he was winning any awards for his acting.

Beyond the childish, class clown, easy-going exterior, Jack was sure that Aaron was a lot more perceptive and aware than he let on.

"It doesn't look like we're gonna succeed at the running or hiding thing," Aaron said as he turned to look at Sophie who was lost in conversation, wildly animated as she spoke. "Which means we need to take the fight to her. Which, I'll be honest with you, bud, I don't exactly look forward to."

"That's what I was afraid of. Fingers crossed, this guy has at least some idea on how to defend ourselves then."

Leaving it at that, they stepped back over to the others who seemed to be winding down in conversation, too.

"We're going in. How do I look?" Rich asked, assuming an outstretched Jesus Christ pose.

"If you're asking if you look like you've recently been stabbed," Aaron said. "Then surprisingly, no. I'd say you look the part."

"Great. I'll try to keep that up. We'll be as swift as we can in there, but you guys stay alert and see what you can get from Victor."

Grace adjusted her jacket at the collar before brushing down the shoulders. "I wish I had a clipboard or something. Okay, let's go."

"Stay safe in there," Sophie called after them as the pair set off towards the imposing steel doors.

CHAPTER 19

Stepping through the prison doors was like entering the visual personification of their current state of being.

The lifeless brick walls were a dismal sky blue in so many layers of paint that it looked like you could peel it from the very stone.

Smooth grey flooring was heavily marred with the tracks of thousands of weeping wives and family members, marching to their bleak hour of visitation granted to them by her majesty's pleasure.

Every aspect of the building was draining to the soul, right down to the harsh fluorescent lighting humming overhead and the clinical, disinfectant smell that burned nostrils as you entered.

In short, this was not a building of rainbows and sunshine. Almost like being here was considered a punishment.

Rich gritted his teeth and tried to walk normally in the face of his pain as he and Grace zeroed in on the front desk and headed over immediately. The less time they gave themselves to panic, the better.

After signing in at the desk and having no choice but to use their real names, they had their identifications checked and were led through into a large waiting room.

Numbered lockers lined the back wall to store keys, phones, wallets, essentially everything one might carry on their person.

Anything could be a weapon, Rich thought as he emptied his pockets into the grey metallic cube.

He was dreading the idea of a pat down, as he didn't think his injury would go unnoticed and was sure that a man with a stab wound trying to get into a prison would raise some serious questions.

Luckily, when it was their time to be called through, the next room was set up much like airport security and they just had to pass through a metal detector, with no hands-on approach at all.

After their final checks they were ushered into a large room with an array of unusual square tables with four legs that curved up from the ground like a Lovecraftian nightmare, ending with circular seats on each end.

The chairs too, it seemed also had to be static to avoid being used as weapons.

The prison guard who'd brought them in gestured to one of the tables and said he'd be back shortly with Johnson.

"We've got this far, so it must mean he's coming," Grace said as she lowered herself down onto the cold metallic seat.

Rich sat down on the table appendage to her right, wincing as his weight shifted. What had been a barely noticeable twinge at first, was becoming more of a constant pain. Maybe it would have been better to send Jack in his place.

"I have no idea on the protocol, but it would seem likely, yeah. Can't see why they'd put us through the gauntlet of checks just to tell us to piss off."

"Would feel like a kick in the tits, that's for sure."

"I'm hoping you've got some idea of what you're going to ask this guy, by the way, because right now all I've got is 'help'."

"Figured I'd tell him there's a nail file in a cake waiting for him if he can give us some decent intel," she snorted.

"Not sure that would work so well for a guy who doesn't seem to want out," Rich said as another twinge of pain fired in his stomach.

A buzzing from across the room preceded the opening of the door as an imposing figure stepped in ahead of the guard.

Though he looked to stand at an average height of about five-nine, what he lacked in height he made up for in muscle.

Even dressed in the prison regulation grey joggers and sweatshirt, it was clear that this man was built from many hours of intense gym time. His neck was as wide as his closely shaven head, and a huge pink scar ran up from below his chin, reaching to the top of his cheek.

He stepped across the room towards them, hands awkwardly thrust out in front of him due to the cuffs on his wrists, and lowered himself down onto a stool, dropping his heavy wrists onto the table with a thud.

"Well," he began, in a voice far softer than either of them had expected.

"Mr Johnson," Grace began, sensing his opening statement was already finished. "Thank you so much for agreeing to meet with us, we have a lot of questions for you and really appreciate your time."

"I do have a rather busy schedule to keep to, but I guess I can miss a session of staring at the ceiling to come and talk to you." His focus was divided between both her and Rich, an unblinking stare that was unnerving to the pair. "The cave?"

"Yes, we had some questions about—"

"We can get to that," he cut her off. "But first, and I know this is going to be difficult given that I'm sure they clipped your wings on the way in, but I'm going to need you both to hurt yourselves."

"Excuse me?" Rich said, looking both intimidated and confused.

"Hang on," Grace said, putting a hand on Rich's shoulder and meeting the man's stare. "I think I follow you. Any injury?"

"Mhmm." He nodded, the thick veins in his neck pulsing as his head bobbed.

"Okay," Grace said as she pulled an odd pensive face for a moment before it transformed into a grimace as she bit into her lower lip, the pain of hurting herself intentionally seemed somehow heightened. She cast a glance over to the guard at the door, who was barely paying attention and then turned her attention back to the man across the table.

Lowering her head slightly, she spat a stringy globule of blood and saliva onto the table, the thick strand of gooey liquid briefly connecting her to the tabletop before she wiped her mouth with the back of her hand.

"Good enough," he said before turning to Rich.

Having brought himself up to speed, Rich lifted the side of his hoodie in the most pathetic striptease and dug a finger into the now visible gash on his stomach, wincing as he swore through gritted teeth.

Another approving nod.

"Okay, then, so you swam in the pool?"

The pair looked at each other, unease spreading across their faces as they turned back to meet his eyes.

"Wait, that's what we did wrong?" Grace said, tonguing the fresh injury inside her bitten lip.

"You swam in her waters and now you're marked. That's what we figured anyway."

"Hang on," Rich said. "Who is she?"

"That," the man paused. "I have no clue. A witch, a demon, some malevolent being that didn't like you stepping foot inside her gingerbread house, God only knows. But once you dipped your toe in that water, you were fucked from then on in I'm afraid."

Grace was busy trying to piece things together but latched on to one key part of his reveal.

"You keep mentioning the water. You're saying that's why she's coming after us? Because two of our group didn't go into the pool. In fact, one wasn't even with us at the cave."

"And she isn't after them. Trust me, one of my group didn't go in the water either, and she didn't go after her." He paused. "Well, not in the same way."

"In what way, then?" Rich asked, feeling the room around him begin to sway.

"Has she possessed either of them yet?"

Blank expressions stared back at him.

"Yeah. In that way." He looked pained as he responded, as if remembering a moment from his past.

"Fuck," Grace hissed through clenched teeth.

"Look, here's all I can tell you. She won't stop coming for you, she can be anywhere, change her shape to look however she wants, bring literally anything to life and can possess people to get to you." He paused again. "Though not anyone that's marked by her pool as far as I can tell."

"So, what's the bad news?" Grace smiled weakly.

"She can hurt you, and only you. I don't know the reasoning, but it seems she can't harm anyone that's not part of this, so public places are your friends. She can't just flip the bus you're on is what I'm getting at."

Right," Rich added. "And stopping her?"

"Fucked if I know, kid." He laughed. "I wouldn't be stuck in here fighting for my life constantly if I did."

"She's still coming after you? It's been how long?" Grace asked.

"Close to thirty years. She doesn't get much chance these days. I've made sure I'm kept away from the rest of neighbours, and they don't trust me with anything in my room anymore. That, and I figured out that all I have to do is hurt whoever she takes control of and she's gone. Part of that not being able to hurt people thing I guess."

"That's still awful," Rich said, realising that this wall of muscle before him was just fighting to stay alive. A flash of understanding hit him. "That's why you made us hurt ourselves. So you knew we weren't being controlled by her."

He nodded. "Just wish I found that part out sooner." Again, his words were steeped with sadness.

"And you definitely don't have any ideas or leads on stopping her at all?" Rich asked again, doing his best to regulate his breathing.

"I'm sorry," the man said. "I wish I did. We tried bricking up the cave, but that didn't do a thing. You're on your own."

"Thank you anyway," Grace said. "You've given us a lot more to work with than we had before. We're probably already dead, but I'm not going down without a fight." Tears glistened in her eyes.

A previously unseen softness seemed to fill the man's face as he smirked at that. "You're feisty. I hope you have better luck than me."

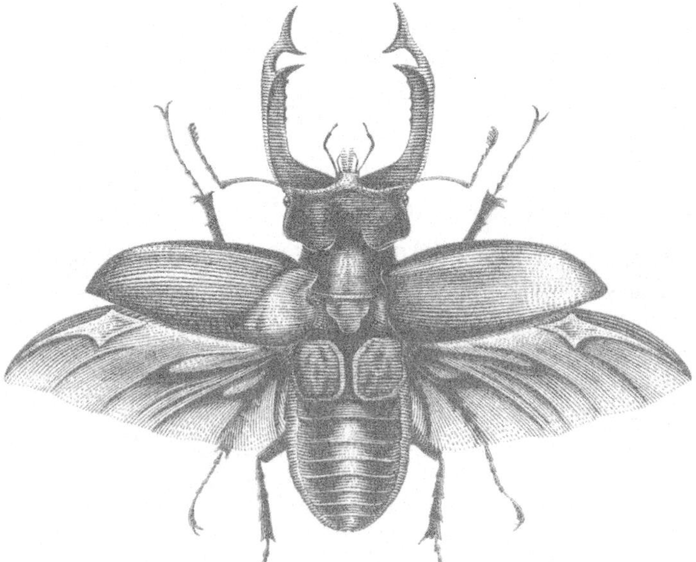

CHAPTER 20

The huge blue doors slowly closed behind them as they left the prison, and being back out in the sunshine brought some welcome relief.

Though their minds were swimming with all the new information they had just picked up, an immediate weight was lifted from their shoulders as they left.

Just being inside that cold, frigid building had sapped all the joy from them.

The contrast of the August summer heat washing over them in a delicate breeze, and the sun's rays gently warming their skin was delightful. A clear, cloudless, blue sky above brightened the late morning, and it was almost enough to make them forget they were being hunted.

Almost.

Making their way over to the cars, they saw that the party was assembled around Jack's Audi, with only Chris still inside, his door open to remain part of the conversation.

Having spotted their return, the group bridged the gap, meeting them partway between both cars.

"From your faces, I assume he turned up and it wasn't exactly all good news," Jack said as they approached.

"Some insights, but not a great deal that we didn't already know," Grace said in response.

"But no fix?" Chris called from his seat in the car.

"Not so much. The guys been fighting to stay alive in there for decades. It looks like it's down to us to figure a way out of this." Rich was modelling a particularly unflattering pallor and was feeling rather green about the gills.

"It's a good job we might have a lead, then," Sophie said as she stepped up to them. "Victor seems to think his grandma might be a wealth of knowledge on some of the stuff in the cave. We figured we'd head right over there now. He's going to meet us there."

"Now?" Rich asked.

"Do you have somewhere else to be?" asked Aaron. "Come on, Jack's got the directions too, we can fill each other in on the way over."

Aaron and Sophie waved to the rest of the group as they moved to their car with Rich and Grace following behind.

Back on the road, the two cars left the prison and its hanging melancholy behind them and soon found themselves back on the country roads pinned by forest on either side.

The high noon sun was baking, and it was beginning to smell pretty ripe inside the cars, the combination of heat, constant movement and lack of showering was building up across the group.

The winding roads were oddly quiet, but meant they were making excellent time. Aaron's Satnav told him there was just fifty-two minutes until arrival. He glanced at the others in his own car and the one behind. No sign of Chris, who was presumably hiding from the sun. A fact that was starting to worry the group, but as yet nobody had voiced their concerns.

Would it even be safe to take him to a hospital right now? And how would they even explain it?

Aaron kept an eye on the road while simultaneously remaining vigilant of his surroundings, the ever-present danger of another appearance from their huntress firmly in the back of his mind.

Once again speeding along towards their destination, the cars aircons blasting and the weather shaping up to be another beautiful summer day, it was easy to forget about the dire, perilous situation that they'd found themselves in.

This was the definition of a living nightmare.

Fleeing from a threat that was both terrifying and unknown with no real light at the end of the tunnel. *They were fucked.*

In his mind there were no two ways about it. This wasn't a movie, and they were not the urbex seven on the run from a hell hag from the caves of death.

Seven.

It stung when he realised how quickly they'd forgotten about Francine. It had been barely twenty-four hours since they'd arrived at her house to be met with a hysterical Dora, puffy eyed, full of snot and barely clinging on to her sanity.

Only yesterday had their ordeal began.

Aaron was no stranger to death. His throat tightened as unwelcome images from his past made their way into his mind. The mangled body of his classmate on the road after being hit by the bus at just twelve years old. His dead grandfather, sprawled peacefully in his bed, waiting to be found by Aaron.

Over the years he'd seen a number of fatalities through traffic accidents, and once he was even on a train that passed over a guy who was obviously at the end of his rope, but none of these had really affected him in a major way.

Death happened.

Francine though, this was a whole new level, and he wasn't afraid to admit it had shaken him up way more than he was letting on.

Yeah, they were definitely fucked.

Sure, he hoped there was some way they could escape or banish their attacker, but right now his focus was of a singular desire. Keep Sophie safe.

With his eyes on the road and head filled with potential incoming threats, he was oblivious to the danger within the car.

Beneath his seat, the snake uncoiled itself and slithered from the darkness.

Five feet of cylindrical muscle writhed and contracted as it raised its head into the footwell of the car. Glistening, iridescent scales coated its body like an oil slick, the vibrant greens and purples blending seamlessly with the chromatic copper and golden scales as it coiled into the light.

Rising like a periscope from the depths of the ocean, the snakes head appeared between the legs of the unaware Aaron, rotating silently as it reared back, jaws opening to reveal rows of needle-like sharp teeth, its forked tongue licking at the air.

The snake's head shot forward, its mouth locking onto Aaron's inner thigh as teeth sank deep into flesh.

He let out a scream as the pain shot through his body and looked down in time to see its jaws unlock and rear back before lunging directly at his face, burying its fangs into his cheek.

With the snake hanging from his face, he panicked and let go of the wheel in an attempt to extract it, as Sophie's screams filled the car.

Shouting from Rich and Grace soon joined the mix as the car spun out of control, jack-knifing left, leaving the road and heading towards the treeline.

The tyres spun on dry earth as the car rotated, slamming side on into a tree, buckling the door inwards as it wrapped around the sturdy oak trunk and shunted its occupants to the right as the impact hit. Glass shattered around them.

Passenger side doors were thrown open as Rich and Sophie fell ungracefully from the car. Aaron ripped the snake from his face, the skin of his cheek burning as a chunk of it was ripped away, and he threw it to his right as he scrambled across the gearstick to join them.

Clambering unceremoniously from the ground in a panicked state, the trio looked back into the car where Grace's body lay slumped, left arm hanging out the door, her head resting face down through the shattered window.

"Fuck!" Rich yelled as he bent to climb back into the car.

"Rich, wait," Aaron said dragging him back. "You can't just pull her out, I'm going to have to go round and lift her head through that window."

Pulse racing, Aaron sprinted round the back of the car and almost ran headlong into worse trouble.

Grace's head lolled out of the window, face down. Her chin rested on the outside of the door, and blood ran down her arm and dripped from her fingers.

Behind the car, with her back to the trunk of the tree, stood the woman from the cave, her ashen hair limply framing a disgusted sneer.

His blood froze as he skidded to a halt and backed up slightly, adding to the distance between them.

Mere seconds of the standoff passed before the woman's lips parted, and a forked tongue lashed quickly over her blood-soaked mouth.

"I was growing tired of this cat and mouse game," her voice purred. It had a coarse, raspy cadence to it, but was oddly seductive. "So, I decided to speed things along."

Aaron stood transfixed by the woman, who was now almost close enough to touch. He heaved at the malodorous stench of rot and stagnant water oozing from her very pores.

She took a step forward, and the dry grass crunched under her bare feet. Resting a hand on the top of Grace's comatose head, she said, "What say we get on with it?"

Aaron's fear mixed with shame as his immediate fight or flight response was of the fleeing variety, but he managed to cement his feet, refusing to break eye contact.

Her eyes fixed on Aaron as a grin spread across her face. The woman's resting hand became a fist, grabbing a handful of Grace's hair and forcing her head downwards, grinding her throat back and forth across the broken glass.

Aaron choked back the vomit that had risen in his throat as he helplessly watched, heaving at the fleshy tearing sound as blood began to gush down the side of the car door.

"I'll fucking kill you!" he screamed, snapping out of his frozen stupor. He lunged, arms shot up in front of him, rage taking up every corner of his mind and body.

But then something forced him backwards, knocking the wind from his chest.

Jack watched the car swerve erratically in front of them, weaving dangerously into the next lane before suddenly careening off to the left, leaving the road altogether.

"We've got fuckery happening," he said, stating the obvious as he readied to pull over where Aaron had left the road.

A second later the car spun and smashed into a large tree, the sound of metal on wood a cacophony of destruction and broken glass.

Jack slammed on the brakes and skidded to a halt on the side of the road, while poor Chris slammed into the back of his seat as the trio were shunted forward with the emergency stop.

Leaving the engine running, he unfastened his seatbelt and put a hand on the door. "Stay in the car, I'm going to make sure everyone is alright."

After stepping out of the car, he moved past the windscreen and gestured to Dora, mouthing *two minutes* as he hesitantly made his way towards the wreckage, wary of potential danger.

In the distance Sophie, Rich and Aaron fell out of the car in a heap, and Jack watched as Aaron rushed around the back of the car.

Grace must be hurt. Jack picked up his pace, panic building inside him.

He watched as Rich moved to follow Aaron round the car and soon heard Aaron screaming something as he appeared again. Rich dragged him backwards as he thrashed in his grip.

What followed next chilled his bones.

The woman appeared from behind the car, her head cocked as she slowly stepped towards them, moving with a delicate grace, each bare foot landing directly in front of the other.

"Guys!" Jack shouted. "Come on, let's go. Now!"

Without realising, he was already stepping backwards as he barked orders, arm waving for them to follow.

Having finally given up struggling to break free of Rich's grasp, Aaron turned to Sophie and screamed for her to run as he and Rich began sprinting behind her towards Jack.

The foursome charged back to the Audi and Jack rushed round to the driver's seat, Dora's horrified face greeting him.

Chris had thrown the back passenger door open and Rich shoved Sophie into the back before climbing in as Aaron dove in across their laps as Rich struggled to close the door, Jack already putting the car into gear.

As soon as they were squashed in, the car moved off, sending dust up into the air as the woman in white patiently continued making her way towards them.

"Shit, shit, shit, shit, shit, shit, shit," Jack repeated as the car picked up speed, checking the rearview mirror to see the woman casually stepping out into the road and stopping to stare at the escaping vehicle.

Muffled shouts from the backseat filled the car as Aaron managed to extract his face from Chris's thighs. "Turn the fuck back around," he spat. "Jack, I'm not joking, turn around. Drive straight into her if you have to, but I'm done running."

Wedged between the boys, Sophie sobbed, and Chris stared coldly at the back of Jack's head, lost in thought, or perhaps locked in the stony silence of fear.

It was Dora who brought them all back to the present. "Aaron's right," she blurted out, an expression of nervous calm on her face as she picked at the skin around her fingernails. "Run the bitch down."

The car screeched to a halt in the road, jerking them all forward.

"Ahh, fuck this," Jack said as he forced the car into reverse and pressed his foot to the floor.

The car began moving backwards, the engine screaming its disapproval as it picked up speed, closing the gap on the woman who stood casually in the road behind them.

"This is a bad idea," Rich said as they got closer and closer to the very person they were running from.

She made no attempt to step aside as they reached her, smiling wickedly at them through the rear window as the car struck her body, sending her underneath with a crunch of metal on flesh as they felt the car go over her.

Jack continued reversing a little further before coming to a stop, the woman's lifeless form a heap in the road before them. He looked to the rest of them in the car, a moment of smug victory passing across his face before turning back to the road.

The body began to rise from the warm tarmac, limbs snapping back into place like a horrifying stop-motion cinema piece, her torso jerking as the arms straightened and she turned towards them, head still hanging limp and crooked before it too snapped back into place and that malicious grin returned, levelled right at them.

"Okay, now we run," Jack said, his voice quivering.

"We're not running," Rich said as calmly as he could. "It's a tactical retreat. We're not done with her, but it was never going to be as simple as running her down. We stick to the plan, find out what Victor knows, and go from there. If I'm gonna die, then I'm going out on my own terms."

"Rich's right," Sophie joined in. "We take the fight to her, but we need to at least have an idea of what we're walking into. We need to find out what her weaknesses are."

Jack put the Audi into gear and began to pick up speed as he again headed straight for her, though this time she calmly stepped out of the road to let them pass, smiling as they sped past her.

The first spots of rain landed on the windscreen as the skies began to darken overhead.

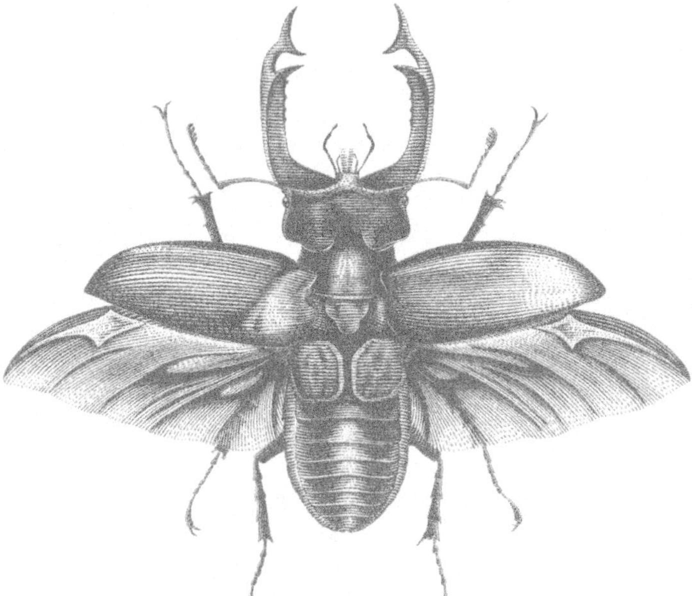

CHAPTER 21

The last leg of their journey brought them back into civilisation, the forests giving way to the concrete jungle.

The weather had swiftly changed as they fled from the scene of the crash, dense grey clouds filling the sky and looming over then in a rainstorm that was meant entirely for them.

Following the directions, they found themselves on a quiet street on the outskirts of the city. Rows of semi-detached houses ran along each side of the street, each with long driveways and tidy gardens.

The torrential rain was keeping people indoors and so their arrival went unnoticed in the neighbourhood.

Wipers clicked rhythmically back and forth over the window as Jack carefully turned into a lengthy driveway, spotting Victor's Moped at the top of the drive, near the house.

"Looks like he's arrived ahead of us at least."

"Does this feel wrong to anyone else?" Dora asked. "Are we not bringing destruction to their door uninvited?"

"She can't hurt anyone else. Only us," Rich said as he wiggled to move Aaron's knee from his crotch.

"What? How do you know that? And would that not be information you could have shared with the rest of us?" Jack snapped.

"Would it have made any difference? And we only just found this out from our prison pen pal. I guess that was part of what we had to discuss when we arrived here."

"Well, I hope you have plenty more nuggets of wisdom for us, Rich," Jack said, as he killed the engine and readied to step out.

The rain hammered down, soaking them to the bone in seconds as they rushed up to the front of the house, constantly checking their surroundings before knocking politely but firmly on the door.

After a few seconds, the sound of movement from inside gave way to the door opening as Victor greeted them, a wide smile across his face that soon diminished as he took in the disarray that was their appearance.

"Friends, please come in, get yourselves out of this deluge."

They piled into the house, single-file, and dripping rainwater as they crowded into the large hallway.

The scent in the air was like a slap to the face from some long forgotten pagan deity – cinnamon, cloves, vanilla, spices of all variety assaulted their nostrils in what felt entirely uncharacteristic of the summer months.

The walls were covered in unusual decorations made of branches and twigs arranged in wreaths and patterns that furthered the autumnal vibe within.

On a side table by the door sat a deep blue ceramic urn, stoppered with a lid complete with a golden design depicting an eagle grappling a snake in its talons.

The same design from the cave. Jack thought.

Victor headed through into the living room, leaving them to drip as they continued to take in their surroundings.

"So, what's this about her not being able to attack anyone else?" Jack asked as soon as Victor left.

"Johnson said she can only go after people who swam in the cave. Apparently, she can possess other people but can't actually harm them, which is why Chris snapped out of it when he got hurt," Rich said a moment before his eyes widened in horrified realisation.

They watched the colour drain from his face as he stumbled backwards, bumping a framed painting on the wall as he managed to catch himself from falling, his ample frame slumped back against the wall.

"Fuck."

"Rich, what is it? Are you okay?" Fear lingered in Sophie's voice.

"The cars. We screwed up." Rich slid down the wall into a crouch and cradled his head in his hands as he continued. "He gave us the information, and we immediately fucked it. Grace is dead because of my ignorance. Oh God."

"What are you talking about? Rich, snap out of it, we don't have time for this." Jack knelt beside him and pulled his hands from his face.

Rich met Jack's eyes, his own now glossy with tears. "The cars, Jack. Up until we left the prison, we had Dora in one and Chris in the other. That's why she didn't come for us then. We left ourselves without a buffer and that cunt took her opportunity."

Aaron raised a fist to punch the wall and stopped himself, as if realising where he was. He drew in a breath, his chest puffing up before he slowly released it. "What's done is done," he said. "We can't change that now, but we have a witch to curb stomp, so can everyone just pull themselves together so we can figure that out?"

"Look," Sophie snapped, centring herself in the cramped hallway and throwing her arms up in the air. "Aaron's right, but we still need to find out what else we can here. It's what we've dragged our butts' miles for, and I can't be the only one that's seen that pot with the design from the cave on it. Grace would want us to try and keep our shit together and find a way to kick this bitch's teeth in, and that's what we're going to do."

As if on cue, Victor put his head around the doorway with a grin. "Friends, my Bunica is ready to speak with you now if you are ready also?"

They stepped through into a large living room filled with furniture that appeared to be older than any of the assembled group. Beige floral sofas, heavy woven wall rugs and hand carved wooden furniture filled every available space inside.

Seated in an equally old and weathered armchair was Victor's grandmother, a woman of considerable age, her olive skin no longer resisting gravity as it slipped from her face like a melting candle. Her wrinkled, yet welcoming face greeted them as they entered, a large mole on her upper lip dancing with her smile. Her once dark hair was mostly grey and what were likely warm brown, beautiful eyes now had a milky coating to them.

Victor knelt beside her and gestured for everyone to take a seat on the sofa's as he gently stroked her hand and spoke softly in Romanian.

With Dora and Chris still struggling to shake off the shock they were dealing with and the guys sitting like awkward schoolboys waiting their turn to be called into the headmaster's office, it was left to Sophie to fill them in on their predicament to date.

Victor's face went through the full range of emotions as she shared their story, stopping her early on to take in the shock news of Francine's death and again for Grace's demise, while his grandmother seemed to take in his swift translation without any visible signs of alarm.

Once she'd finished recounting events, she sat patiently as Victor spoke to his grandmother, conversing back and forth in conversation that was completely unintelligible to her.

After their brief chat, she spoke two words, seemingly for the whole room.

"Vrajitoare furtuna."

Everyone sat forward in their seats, puzzled expressions on their faces as Sophie looked to Victor for clarification.

"It means storm witch," he said. "She says they are well known legends from our country, as well as the surrounding areas."

"The shoe fits," Rich said as he fingered the gash on his stomach.

"She says they were great demons that controlled the skies and caused storms that would destroy crops and farms. Sometimes she appeared as a witch or monster that was said to steal away and eat babes, though this is all folklore, so how much of that is fact is hard to say."

"Well, there's definitely a little more to it than folklore it would seem," Jack interjected.

"Does she know how we can stop her?" Sophie asked.

He turned to his grandmother and continued the conversation in Romanian as they waited, the tension heavy in the room.

"She says that their tradition is to…" he broke off as he struggled to find the word, making a scooping motion with an invisible bowl or bucket.

"Capture?" Rich offered.

"Yes! To capture some rain in the jug to protect your household. You will see I did so just before in the jug by the front door."

"The blue urn with the symbol on it? And that is supposed to keep her locked out?" Sophie said as she was trying to piece things together.

"That is correct. Old superstition, or so I thought."

"And do you think if someone were to do that to a hole in a cave it would maybe trap the witch inside?"

"I do not know, but it sounds like what you have seen."

Rich cleared his throat. "So, say someone managed to turn a cave into a giant container, do you think they could perhaps trap her completely? That sort of feels like what this is." He rubbed at his stomach wound as he paused for a moment. "And then with us disturbing the water, she's able to leave and come after us, but only us it would seem."

Victor scratched his head, seeming to weigh up this new information. "I can't say I have any idea about that, but it sounds like what you are going through, yes."

"Okay, and what about actually hurting her? We need a way to fight her," Aaron said.

Victor turned again to ask in Romanian.

"We call them fingerstein, they are…," he paused again. "Long and like the old bones of the dinosaur?"

"Fossils?" said Rich again.

"I think so yes. They appear from the ground after a thunderstorm and were believed to be lightning from the sky."

His grandmother began speaking to him again and after another brief back and forth, he excused himself.

"One moment."

He reappeared after a short time carrying a spear-like object, about nine inches in length, the colour of orange coral with dark, charcoal patterning across it.

"This is what I mean."

"It looks…" Rich got up and moved to inspect the object. "Like a fossilised spike from a mollusc or some sort of sea creature. And that's supposed to work?"

"So my Bunica says, but this again is from folktales, not personal experience."

"Everything else seems to be ringing true so far," Sophie said.

"Apart from eating babies," Aaron added.

"Maybe that's how she spends her downtime," Jack said. He glanced down at the mysterious weapon. "Victor, can we borrow that?"

"Yes, I think it's important that you do."

CHAPTER 22

After some time passed, in which tea was offered and everyone tried to grasp at a brief period of normality, the storm outside abated to little more than a drizzle.

Whether this was due to her disappearance or to lull them into a false sense of security, none of them could say, but nobody was going to chance peeking their head outside to find out.

Victor had since helped his grandmother up the stairs to lie down and said he would be sitting with her a while, but to help themselves to anything they liked from the kitchen, leaving them to formulate some kind of plan.

"So, we're agreed then?" Jack paced back and forth across the room, adding even further wear to the already threadbare carpet.

"Head back to the cave and break those symbols off the roof," Rich said. "And if she is trapped, hopefully she will fuck off and leave us alone."

"And if she interferes along the way we stick her with this prehistoric squid dick," Aaron added, jabbing the air with the fossil to make his point.

"Something like that, yeah." Jack moved to the window and peered around the blinds into the waterlogged street.

"Releasing her from her prison might get her off our back, but are we not unleashing her on the rest of the world then?" Sophie added.

The thought chilled Rich. "Maybe, but we don't actually know she's that malevolent when she's not caged. This could be just another force of nature in the world that we're completely oblivious to for the most part. Plus, we can't just sit down and wait to die."

From the corner of the sofa, Chris cleared his throat to speak. "I'm not going."

Aaron's head spun so fast he risked whiplash. "You're what? Oh, you rat bastard little shithouse."

"Aaron, chill it." Rich stood up, ready for drama.

"You said it yourself, Rich, she's not after me, it doesn't make any sense for me to go and throw myself at her." Chris looked uncharacteristically steeled in his decision, something that caught them all off guard.

"That's your answer? It doesn't affect you, so fuck the rest of us, is that it?"

"We can't make him go," Jack said. "And while I agree it's a cowardly decision, he has got a point. Dora should stay, too. In fact, maybe both the girls should stay here."

"Yeah, sure, you go off into the lion's den and we'll sit around here making daisy chains and waiting for our periods to line up. Get bent, Jack. I'm coming with." Sophie piped up, giving him the finger.

"I'm going, too," Dora said with a weak smile.

Jack's eyes narrowed as he gave her a concerned father look. Rich knew where he was coming from, and he felt the same. She had, rightly so, been in and out of a practically catatonic state since they'd arrived at Francine's place, and he couldn't see any reason to put her in further harm's way.

"Dora, you don't have to come with us, like Rich said, she's not after you, you can stay here."

"No, I can't. It doesn't matter if she's after me or not, she killed Francine and Grace. I'm in this till the end." She brushed her hair back behind her ears as she stood up from the sofa. "And besides, you need me, I'm your only way of getting a car safely to that cave remember."

"She's got a point," Aaron said. "Especially if Chris is going to sit here pissing his pants instead."

"Get fucked, Aaron." Chris spat.

"Whatever, you'd only be a liability. Stay here, the girls have got more balls than you anyway."

Aaron dropped heavily back onto the sofa like a stroppy teen and Sophie rested her head on his shoulder, nuzzling into his neck.

"you're not going to try and talk me into staying, then?"

"What good would that do? We both know you'd tell me to shove it like you did Jack."

She kissed his cheek, carefully avoiding the grazes across his face. "you're learning. I like that."

Rich shuffled in his seat trying to put some space between himself and the mushy display of affection, but just found himself hanging over the side of the sofa.

He pondered the situation and found himself smiling.

A lifetime of never fitting in, a complete lack of interest in romantic dalliances, and finally landing a windfall that enabled him to shut himself away from the rest of the world. Yet here he was, on the precipice of what would likely be the death of him, and he couldn't think of anyone else he'd rather be with as he marched forward to his demise.

CHAPTER 23

They gathered up, their shadows darkening the boot of the car in Victor's driveway as they stared at their readied supplies. Rich felt a stirring of something akin to excitement building inside of him.

A well-used claw hammer with a black rubber grip, rust covered chisel, three-foot crowbar, two large black torches, two headlamp torches and a metallic first-aid box.

"Not exactly the greatest arsenal in the land," Aaron said, the fossilised spike gripped firmly in hand.

"No, but probably about as much use as anything else would be," Jack said. "You've likely got the only thing that might be a threat, and even that's just a guess right now."

"It's not about killing her; it's fending her off until we get to the cave," Rich added, surprised that his recent surge of bravery still hadn't wilted.

Jack closed the boot of the car as they stepped back, and a round of appraising looks were shared between them. "Then we just have to pray that the plan actually works. I'll be honest, I'm not feeling particularly positive about the whole thing, but it looks like the best shot we've got."

"Better to go out swinging than be hunted down one by one though," Aaron added.

"Ooh ooh, my turn," Sophie chimed in. "Let's take the fight to her. High-five, muscle flex, macho man Randy Savage." Her tongue stuck out as she gagged and rolled her eyes at the boys.

"Hey!" Jack said as he playfully shoved her. "If anything, what I said was self-deprecating."

"Yeah, but look at you, dude. You're a walking Calvin Klein ad." Aaron joked.

Rich walked to the house where Victor leaned in the open doorway, still seemingly quite aloof.

"Victor, please thank your Bunica for all her help, and thank you too for letting us drop all this on you, we all really appreciate it, we'd seriously be lost without you."

"It is the least I can do. I would go with you to this cave if you would let me," he said, and there wasn't even the slightest part of Rich that didn't believe him.

"I know, and that's why we won't let you. You've done more than enough for us and hopefully we will see you soon." He placed a hand on Victor's shoulder and smiled weakly.

"Dora," Rich called. "Last chance. Sure you don't want to stay here?"

"Not a chance, Rich," she replied.

A moment later Chris stepped out of the door past Victor. "Please be careful, guys."

"Get fisted by a sandpaper glove, Chris," Aaron shouted, throwing him both middle fingers. "If I die, I swear I'm gonna haunt you like a motherfucker."

"Guys, come on, save the anger, okay? Let's just get this show on the road." Rich headed towards the car, manifesting confidence, though in reality he didn't think the likelihood of them all surviving to the end of the day was great.

The journey though long, was uneventful. The blue skies and summer sun had returned, making the storm they had holed up in seem like a thing of the past.

Rich glanced beside him at Jack, who was driving, and noted the determination in his friend's eyes. Aaron, Sophie, and Dora were crammed in the back chatting away and for a moment it would be easy to forget the situation they were in - Piled inside Jack's Audi on the way to face their fears and hopefully rid themselves of the sword of Damocles that hung over them.

The whole drive was almost idyllic. Green, serene and lacking any of the imminent threat of death that they had become quickly accustomed to. Even the tiring and sweaty hike back over the hill towards the forest only had them mildly on high alert.

Rich was surprised how quick and easy their ascent was this time round, and figured they were perhaps all running on adrenaline right now.

Reaching the other side of the hill, the familiar forest stretched out ahead of them, the trees so tightly packed that even with the sun high in the sky there was an ominous darkness shrouding its depths.

"Everyone take a breather, down some water and get ready for the next leg," Jack sounded off like a drill sergeant. "Same rules as always, see something fucky, you sound off and run. If you can't run, then make sure you've got your weapons handy."

Rich coughed loudly as he cleared his throat. "Also, and I guess this is a weird time, but if you make it out of this in one piece, I'll give each of you a hundred grand."

"And I'll get everyone a pony," Aaron added.

"I'm serious," Rich said, keeping his face sterner than any of them had ever seen. "I mean it. We don't know how this is going to go, but please none of you go and die on me." He swallowed, realising again how important each of them had become to him.

"What the fuck, Rich?" Aaron playfully shoved him. "I knew you were a drug dealer!"

Rich chuckled. "I'm not, but I've got money, alright? And I mean it, just stay alive for me."

"Here I was planning to die." Dora laughed. "But I guess if there's money in it, I might as well try to stick around."

"Funny. I just mean be careful, ok."

Jack drained the rest of his water, crunching the plastic bottle in his fist as he finished. "Guess we should get on with it then, no time like the present."

With crowbar in hand, he stepped into the depths of the forest as the others followed behind.

The foreboding nature of the woods made itself known as soon as they crossed its threshold – The immediate drop of temperature, if only by a couple of degrees, the creeping darkness, and most alarming, the bubble of sound they found themselves in immediately.

The sounds of hikers and families travelling on the main path could still be heard, but it was somehow muted and far away. A rogue child's laughter sounding much further than the handful of seconds travel it must surely be.

In the distance, the high, rasping buzz of a motorcycle could be heard somewhere in the hills.

Keeping the mountain to their right they ventured further into the depths of the forest. This time around, the shadowy woodlands felt exponentially more sinister, knowing their destination.

Moving through the tightly packed trees, their dry, desiccated trunks aged with rot, it felt like nothing but rows and rows of the same view for miles in every direction, hopeless and never ending.

The dank smell of rot permeated their surroundings and the deafening silence of their wooded enclosure had them shuffling along in a state of tense unease.

Silently shuffling along in single file, Jack at the head of the group, each of them scanned their surroundings for signs of danger.

Periodically out of the corner of his eye, Rich swore he could see the briefest flashes of white passing behind the trees that ran parallel with their journey, momentary glimpses of the woman in white disappearing from view as though she was keeping pace with them as they travelled. Glancing around at the others, he could see their heads too were darting about in a twitchy manner, and knew he wasn't the only one aware of it.

More than once, Aaron wordlessly darted sideways and stepped into the next clearing of trees, his fossilised spear readied to lunge and yet finding nothing more than the continuous spread of forest ahead of him.

A rustling of leaves up high drew Dora's attention where she shared a momentary stand-off with a large black bird nestled on a thick tree branch, curiously cocking its head at her as she stood fixed in place, the penetrating stare of a woman deep in the throes of fear meeting the bird's soulless, beady eyes. Rich wondered how she was coping. The loss she'd suffered must have felt unbearable.

With an unnatural shudder and neck twitch, she blinked hard and shook her head, her feet moving again as she shortened the gap between herself and Sophie ahead of her.

Rich craned his head around as he carefully stepped over some gnarled roots, twisting up from the earth. "Does this feel more—"

"Deadly?" Aaron cut him off.

"I was going to say ominous, but kinda, yeah."

"It feels like it should be foggy," Aaron added, twisting to check on the girls behind them and receiving an out-of-place smile from Sophie.

"It does feel like we're displaced somehow," Jack joined in as he slowed to keep pace. "It even feels cooler than it should be."

"Something about it just feels off. Theres a lull that feels like we're being given a false sense of security," Rich said as he gripped the hammer and chisel tightly in his fists.

"You're not wrong," agreed Jack. "We're in the middle of nowhere. It feels like the perfect time to attack. What's she waiting for?"

"The right time," Dora said from the rear of the group, a smile slowly spreading across her face.

Like lightning, a sinuous thorn coated vine sprang from the undergrowth and wrapped around Jack's leg, coiling three times from ankle to thigh, biting into his flesh as it snapped tight and dragged him from his feet with a scream.

Mere seconds later, three more vines darted from the earth, directly at the guys.

Two of the thorny tendrils shot at Aaron and wrapped his wrists like razor wire as the barbs sunk into flesh and lifted him helplessly from the ground by the arms.

At the same time, the third, more girthy vine whipped around Rich's torso, encircling his body multiple times before also raising him from the ground. His stomach plummeted and fear gripped him as he stared at the shocked faces of each of his friends. They didn't deserve this.

Sophie screamed and tried to run, dashing east and making it about twenty feet before both ankles were caught in snares of thorns, dropping her face first to the ground and splitting her lip on a rock before hoisting her ankle first up into the air.

Dora stood patiently watching as the foursome were raised upwards, dangling a few feet from the forest floor, their viney restraints waving rhythmically like serpents as they displayed their trophies.

A gravelly voice silenced the screams as Dora's lips parted.

"Shall we begin?"

CHAPTER 24

Dora's foot squelched as she stepped in the puddle of water, thick with globules of gelatinous red ichor, the crimson lumps stretching like the layer of skin on old soup before bursting apart between her toes.

Dora screwed up her face. *Why was she barefoot?*

The cloying swamp water stench hung in the air of Francine's kitchen, assaulting Dora's nose as she took in the scene around her.

Dimly lit by only the light from the moon, the room was cast in shades of green as the glow forced itself through the window like an ethereal spotlight.

Dora forced herself to look down at the body she knew to be splayed on the ground before her, her heart already breaking all over again.

Francine's pale body lay on the floor, her arms at unfeasible angles where the bone protruded from her forearms. The back of her head rested against the cupboard below the sink, angled in a way that her lifeless eyes stared straight up at Dora. The craterous hole in her stomach seemed to pulse as what was left of her organs pumped blood out of the hole, running over the side of her body and joining the puddle below.

A hollow rasping filled the silence as Dora watched the now icy blue lips part slightly as the laboured words of Francine began.

"You …" The word was dragged out, a whispering hiss. "… let me die."

This isn't happening.

"No!" Dora bellowed, her eyes filling with tears. "This isn't real. It's not happening, I've already lived out this fucking nightmare."

She began to move back, her wet feet slapping the cool tiles as she stepped away from Francine's corpse.

"I know I'm not really here," she started again, finding the resolve inside herself. "You're in my head, you sick bitch, and I'm not going to lie down and take it."

As she continued staggering backwards towards the door, the kitchen window exploded inwards, sending shards of glass flying across the room, carried on the gale force winds that rushed towards her like a vacuum.

The wind slammed into her and forced her off her feet, flying backwards through the doorway as darkness closed around her.

She landed on her arse with a gasp as she caught her breath. The wind was suddenly gone, and she blinked hard before taking in her new poorly lit surroundings.

Some sort of cave.

With her back still resting against the damp, moss covered rock she'd struck, she carefully stood to her feet and gazed about.

She was standing in a dome shaped grotto with a large body of water at its centre. Flaming sconces lined the walls at regular intervals, providing limited visibility within the huge cavern, and in the far corner a number of large wooden cages, roughly constructed and bound with thick yellowed rope, sat empty.

A repeating, solitary drip, drip, drip of water into the pool was the only sound echoing throughout the cave for about thirty seconds before the screaming began.

The regimented sound of many footsteps in unison carried from the tunnel leading into the cave, getting louder by the second and bringing with it the owner of the terrified screams.

Figures in dark, hooded robes began to spill from the tunnel, parting left and right to allow the continuation of their march to enter the cavern.

Soon after, two weary and frightened looking people were pushed from the tunnel by force. A man and a woman, aged somewhere in their twenties and clad in dirty linen clothing that looked centuries out of date, had both their wrists bound together by thick, hempen rope.

The woman dropped to her knees, sobbing into her hands as her greasy blonde hair stuck to her face. The dark-haired man stood solemn by her side, resting his bound hands upon her shoulder as she wept.

Dora panicked as the hooded figures filled in around them before realising that if they were able to see her, they would have done so by now. She crouched beside the large rock to her side and continued to watch.

A rising ominous chant started throughout the crowd as four of the men stepped towards the pair, and grabbing them by the arms, began to haul them in the direction of the pool.

Screams and shouts filled the cavern, overpowering the chants as the pair struggled to break free from their restraints and force themselves back, heels digging into the dirty ground.

It was to no avail, and they were dragged on their knees to the edge of the pool where the men stopped. One of the robed figures stepped forward and pulled back their hood to reveal a balding, grey-haired man with a short salt and pepper beard and mean, wrinkled face, weathered by many years.

"Cast the betrayers into the water." His voice, though nasal, carried a regalness that obviously commanded respect.

Amid more screams, the pair were flung into the pool with a splash as they sank underneath the lichen-coated water for a few seconds before breaking the surface again with fearful gasps as they filled their lungs with air.

Like rats from a sinking ship, they floundered, hands still bound, towards the water's edge and heaved themselves ungracefully back out onto the cave floor where they lay, soaked to the bone and breathing heavily.

The robed figures watched on as after a time the pair struggled to their feet and cast terrified glances around at the assembly before them, unsure what was to happen next.

The bearded man broke the silence.

"You can go now, children. Though I suggest you make haste." He gestured broadly with his arm as the crowd of men parted to let the pair pass.

Without a moment's hesitation, the duo darted through the opening and fled as fast as their legs could carry them, soon disappearing into the tunnel, only the trail of water they dropped behind them giving any indication they were ever there.

What is going on?

Dora had no idea what she was bearing witness to and was beginning to put together a series of questions in her head when the waters began to stir.

Breaking the surface in a steady movement towards the water's edge, a head slowly emerged from the pool, dark hair clinging to the emaciated yellowed flesh of a withered woman. Vile and evil looking, this was every bit the archetype of what Dora expected a witch to look like.

As she continued to move forwards, rising higher from the surface of the water, her body, naked for all but a leathery animal hide loincloth, came into view. As sickly and malnourished as the face, rough leathery skin coated the frail looking body that was wrinkled and pock marked with brown spots. The breasts hung like empty sacs; bold blue veins visible across them.

Dora gagged at the jagged, yellow toenails as the woman stepped out onto the cave floor, and the malodorous stench of rot that she brought with her carried right across the cave to where she cowered.

The man cleared his throat, showing no sign that the rancid smell was bothering him as he spoke again.

"My lady, the hunt is on. Please see to it that these traitors are dealt with accordingly."

The look of disgust she gave the man was in no way disguised but soon turned into a grinning sneer as Dora watched the witch slowly begin to transform before her eyes.

The flesh began to tighten and contract, and bones seemed to snap as she straightened up, gaining in height. The once yellowed flesh became a smooth blue-grey and her hair became a flowing mane of white, spun silk.

In moments, the hag before her had transformed into an otherworldly goddess of cold beauty, though the hatred still radiated from her like a force unto itself.

Transfixed by this change, Dora watched on in horror as the woman slowly turned towards her, a smile widening across her face as she locked eyes with her.

"Fuck this, I need to wake up." Dora broke the stare and looked about the cave.

Deciding she had nothing to lose, she bolted to her left and cast her forearm into the open flame of the torch on the wall, pain flaring up her arm as the smell of scorched flesh filled the cavern.

CHAPTER 25

Jack, hanging painfully from one leg was exerting all the effort he could as he tried to bring himself upright towards his vine-wrapped restraint, a feat of strength that was far beyond anyone else in the group.

Aaron, meanwhile, was busy screaming at both Sophie and Dora, a mix of caring encouragement and venomous vitriol.

For her part, Sophie had bypassed the screams and moved straight into the pained and panicked sobs of the resigned.

With three quarters of their group suspended upside down, blood rushing to their heads and thorny vines biting into their flesh as the now malevolent looking Dora stepped slowly forward, it was only Rich, still upright in his bindings, that could clearly see the figure rapidly approaching in the distance.

Evil Dora turned just a moment too late as the red faced and sweat-soaked man rushed towards her, closing the gap and arcing out a swing from his arm, heaving the odd black device across her as a burning pain ignited her flesh.

Rich's eyes widened. *Chris?*

A blood-curdling scream filled the clearing as Dora dropped to her knees, clutching her forearm tightly, and the restrained foursome lurched as their vine-like captors dropped them two feet closer to the ground.

Not wasting a moment, Chris dashed forward and raised the blowtorch to Rich's restraints, the arc of flame immolating the vine in seconds and dropping him heavily to the forest floor.

After helping him up, they moved to Sophie, and Rich pulled her down by her armpits as Chris repeated the destruction of her restraints.

Continuing in the same manner, they soon had Aaron and Jack freed.

"Chris, what the fuck?" Aaron blurted as he shoved Chris hard enough for him to stumble.

"Thought you were sitting the rest of this out?" Jack said as he positioned himself between the pair.

Chris, still red in the face, was puffing heavily as he tried to compose himself. "I had to say that. I've got no idea how much she could see."

"Explain," Dora added, seemingly snapped back into her reality as she sat on the ground, rummaging through the first-aid kit.

"I knew we needed supplies, and I figured if she's not after me, I'd have the freedom to go and get some unhindered. I left with Victor the moment you guys were out of sight," Chris said as he began to shrug off the large, blue backpack that they hadn't noticed.

The look of shock and bewilderment was plastered on all their faces.

"We went to get some stuff and I had Victor run me straight here on his bike. I made him drop me off and turn back once we'd made it as far as the forest, though. It was already asking too much of him."

Chris opened the backpack and began retrieving items from inside.

"We've got the blowtorch, and another can of fuel, a couple of hatchets and a couple of hammers," he said as he laid out the tools before him on the ground.

"Damn, Chris," Jack said as he took in the array of black tools in front of them.

"Carbon steel," he said. "Didn't think it was the time to cheap out on stuff."

Aaron cleared his throat, more for effect than requirement and spoke. "Chris, I won't apologise for what I said when I thought you were abandoning us, but I'm glad I was wrong. You've probably just saved our lives."

Dora finished bandaging her arm as best she could and moved to Sophie, who was still slumped on the ground gently sobbing. "You okay, chick?"

Sophie looked up, tears smearing her face, a combined expression of sadness and shame.

"I just ..." she started and felt the lump catch in her throat. "I just wanted to see a ghost. You know, it seemed cool, but I didn't want this. Are we going to die? This feels too much, it's not fair."

Dora nodded and frowned for a moment before she spoke. "I've got a brother you know. He's nineteen, but I swear he's the wisest little shit I've ever met." She paused again waiting for Sophie's full attention before she continued. "He says the world's full of assholes. And do you know why?"

Sophie sniffed. "Why?"

"Because we let them be. Because nobody ever puts them in their place and so they carry on acting that way."

"Is there a point coming?"

"Well, she's doing this because she can. So maybe we're the ones who are supposed to show her that she can't. Even if we fail, maybe we can have enough of an impact that she'll think twice before doing it again."

"He sounds really smart," Sophie smiled. "Got a lot of experience with murderous swamp hags, has he?"

Dora laughed. "No, I can't say he has, but let's just say there are enough regular people out there that are filled with hatred."

"I'm sure he's very proud of his big sister. Thanks for the pep talk, I needed it." She raised herself off the ground and brushed herself off. "Now let's go kill this witch."

CHAPTER 26

Newly re-grouped and armed, they continued onwards towards the cave, fear and trepidation weighing heavily with each step.

"Like a demonic homing missile?" Rich asked as he tried to make sense of Dora's bombshell.

"I guess so," Dora confirmed. "Like I said, I was stuck in a memory like Chris was, but I shook it off. Next thing I know I'm in some creepy fucking cave and a bunch of medieval pricks in robes are chucking a couple into the water. They flop out and do a runner and then she comes creeping out of the water like some undead James Bond femme fatale, and this bearded arsehole sends her after them."

"So maybe this cult captured her in the cave and the water is like a death sentence," Sophie chimed in. "That's one way to hand out executions I suppose."

"This would explain why she can come for us but is otherwise trapped in there then. Adds weight to the idea that setting her free might get us off the hook." Rich said, though he felt he had none of the bravery to back up his statement.

"Set her free or die trying. Got it. Let's just get to the cave." Aaron said.

Aaron and Jack took the lead with Sophie and Rich at the rear, keeping the two susceptible members of the party in the middle where they could keep an eye on them.

Aaron swung the newly acquired axe in the air, testing its weight as he gripped the fossilised spike in his off hand.

Chris too gripped tightly to an axe, the blowtorch ready in his left, though his dour expression showed he wasn't nearly as confident in moving forward as the others.

The two new graphite hammers had been shared between Sophie and Dora, leaving Rich with the original hammer and chisel that he'd set out with and Jack with the large crowbar.

Everybody was alert and weapons were drawn ready to be used at a moment's notice.

They didn't think they'd be waiting long.

And they were correct.

Through the clearing of trees ahead of them stepped four shambling creatures. A blighted marriage of gnarled and twisted branches, woven and intertwined into some semblance of humanoid shape.

A toxic green glow emanated from the narrow gaps between branches and served as make-shift eyes. Sharp, thorny edges jutted from their heads and parts of their bodies. Hollow mouths of jagged spines opened and closed menacingly as they silently approached.

"What in the fucking demon Groot are they?" Aaron spat as he raised his axe ready to attack.

"The welcoming party," Jack said. "Pretty sure just restraining us isn't going to be their plan of attack, so don't hold back.

They were now collectively battered, bruised, burnt and bleeding, and it was no surprise that the idea to try and run wasn't floated by a single one of them.

Patience was wearing thin and at this stage they all knew their destination, and that the only way to get there was through whatever was thrown at them.

As the creatures ambled forward like sinister scarecrows, splayed feet of many roots stomping heavily as they moved, Aaron and Jack charged to meet them, weapons raised high. The others closed the gap behind them.

Jack swung the crowbar with both hands as the creature lashed out a thorny claw in his direction, bringing the crowbar down with all his might onto the wooden arm, splintering branches as it landed.

Aaron's axe sunk deeply into what he considered the neck of the monster before him, separating the twisted vines as it carved deeply into its body. Unfortunately for him, that was where it got stuck, lodged into the body of the beast, leaving him struggling to pull it free as sharp claws lashed out in his direction.

A hammer shattered the incoming hand as Sophie arrived, a screaming battle cry punctuating the blow which she followed up with another strike to the creature's face, cracking the unnatural, wooden teeth inwards and sending the thing toppling backwards, Aaron's axe freeing itself as it fell.

They both descended on the toppled creature and mercilessly rained hammer and axe blows upon it, smashing it to pieces as fragments of wood began to fly around them.

Not thinking straight, Dora threw the hammer in her grip at another of the tree-like horrors as she rushed forward alongside Chris, luckily hitting it square in the midsection and causing it to stagger backwards affording Chris the time to dart towards it and hit it with a blast from the blowtorch, igniting it immediately.

Dora recovered her hammer, and they watched as the monster staggered about wildly, a deadly living bonfire, before turning their attention to the final creature heading in their direction.

Seeing Aaron and Sophie savagely dismantling their foe, and the other two swiftly incinerating and moving onto another, Rich rushed to help Jack, who was enthusiastically raining blows upon his target.

He arrived in time to see Jack catch the full weight of a trunk-like arm across the face, sending him to the ground, and dashed forward with his hammer raised.

Rich brought the hammer down onto the face of the creature, and the loud splitting of wood echoed around him as a shockwave of pain ran up his arm.

Barely registering the blow, the thing lashed out a jagged claw of wooden shards that cut across Rich's body, tearing through fabric and leaving a row of shallow lacerations on his chest.

He roared in pain as he fell away from the attack, landing heavily on his arse and immediately shuffling backwards as the thing loomed towards him. Another of its brethren went up in flames behind it.

Rich felt the bile rising in his throat and his heart raced as the creature brought another claw up to strike as it moved towards him.

The arm snapped like a wishbone as Jack brought the crowbar down on it, leaving the lower half dangling from broken vines. He followed up with another two-handed strike across the creature's chest, forcing it back as he gave Rich the time he needed to scrabble to his feet.

"You good?" he called over his shoulder as he planted himself between Rich and the tree monster.

"Define good," Rich replied as he moved to Jack's side. "I'm not dead yet, if that's what you mean."

"Good enough," Jack said as he narrowed his eyes at the monster before them. "Let's finish this."

He shot forward and swung the crowbar at the creature's remaining arm, missing by inches as it lashed out a wide swing that arced across just inches from his face.

Stepping to his right, he leaned in, swinging low at the thing's leg, allowing Rich to move in from the left.

The impact of the blow did nothing to the solid trunk of tree that was its leg, but the resonating shock that ran through his arms staggered him for a second.

The thing lunged forward, throwing all its weight into the remaining arm, and buried its claws deeply into Jack's chest, gnarled and splintered fingers ripping through skin and muscle as it toppled down onto him.

Pinned below it, Jack groaned hoarsely as the jagged wooden spikes buried themselves into the flesh below his collarbone, twisting and writhing as the creature forced them deeper.

Howls of pain filled the forest as Jack tried to push the thing off him, its rough, bark-like scraping skin like sandpaper against his free hand.

The crushing pressure was released as the thing was lifted from him, its stake-like fingers coming free with chunks of flesh still attached as Rich, Aaron, and Sophie dragged it from his pinned body and heaved it aside. Chris arrived just in time to spray it with fire.

It fell to the forest floor, writhing as the flames quickly engulfed its body, lapping at the dried wood and burning it up, leaving just the smell of charred wood filling the air.

Rushing to Jack's aid, the group circled around him, and Rich lifted him up slightly and pulled him onto his lap.

"We need to dress his injuries," Dora shouted as she fell to her knees and snapped open the first aid kit.

Aaron knelt and ripped the already torn fabric away from the wound, wincing at the sight of the mangled and shredded skin beneath, blood running from the punctured flesh.

"That bad then?" Jack coughed, smiling weakly up at Aaron.

"It'll be fine, we just need to get some pressure on it and get you patched up."

Jack narrowed his eyes at Aaron, unimpressed by the obvious attempt at a lie.

"You've got a truly awful poker face, mate."

"Stop it," Rich snapped, pulling his hoodie off and remembering the cuts on his own chest briefly before balling it up and handing it to Aaron to try stop Jack's bleeding. "You're gonna be fine."

"No, I'm not. But that's alright, I went down fighting, that's all I can ask for," Jack said as he ran his tongue over his teeth, collecting the blood in his mouth.

"You need to push on," he continued. "And you know she's going to push back, but you need to get there and make her pay. Don't let us die for nothing."

Grief filled Rich's chest and he bit hard on the inside of his mouth to keep himself from sobbing.

Jack's breathing was beginning to sound more and more laboured, and he was sniffing as he spoke, as if choking back fluid.

The time for denial had passed and it was evident on all their faces.

"You can't…" he coughed; the energy slowly being sapped from his body. "…sit around here. She's not… gonna give you a chance to rest."

Another cough brought forth a spatter of blood, drooling over his lower lip. "Go."

A wet, choking gurgle filled Jack's throat, ending with a swallow and then silence.

That sound would haunt them for the rest of their days.

Sophie broke down and dropped to her knees in heavy sobs, her body heaving with emotion.

Rich gently stood up, lowering Jack's head to the ground as Aaron draped the blood-soaked hoodie across his chest.

Aaron said as he cast a glance around the smouldering corpses of the tree creatures. "He's right. We need to move, but this whore dies today."

CHAPTER 27

Tromping onwards through the forest was beginning to take its toll on the exhausted group. The densely packed trees, while refusing to let the sunlight through, seemingly had no issues allowing the summer heat to slowly bake them as they walked.

Marching forward, heads hung low and carrying the weight of Jack's recent passing, they were all running on fumes.

Stomachs roiled and churned as they sat empty, their last proper meals feeling like a lifetime ago. The pulsing dehydration headaches and throbbing pain of a variety of injuries a constant reminder of how deep in they were.

Rich fingered the shallow gashes on his chest, packed deep with a salve Dora had procured from the first-aid kit, and winced as the hot stinging pain resonated through him. The throbbing from the slash in his stomach joined the party and added to his discomfort.

Aaron looked like something out of a nightmare, the series of cuts and grazes that covered his body oozing and bleeding weakly, covering him in enough blood to give Carrie and her prom night mishap a run for her money.

The sudden appearance of a strong wind was like a heavenly kiss as it ran over them, its cooling breeze invigorating and refreshing.

Sophie wiped the sweat from her brow with the back of her sleeve and puffed out a breath, forcing the sweat slicked hair from her face. "Does this feel like it's taking longer to get to than last time to anyone else?"

"Hard to say," Rich said, struggling to keep pace with the group, his cheeks flushed and sweaty. "I hadn't been stabbed last time we made the trip."

"Right?" Aaron laughed, probably glad for the moment of levity. "I'm not sure if I'm more covered in blood or sweat—"

"Sweat," chorused Sophie and Dora.

"I think I just need the tears and I'm the full package."

"I'm pretty sure we're getting close," Chris said as he craned his head skyward, staring past the trees at the side of the mountain.

Rich opened his mouth to respond when something hit the back of his throat.

A buzzing speck of movement danced off his tonsils, whirring around the inside of his mouth, causing him to panic, gag and retch as he doubled over, choking out a weak amount of bile and water onto the forest floor.

"Guhh … I think I just swallowed a fly."

Aaron started to laugh at the spectacle when the buzzing began.

The monotonous drone filled the air as a blanket of moving darkness descended upon them, blocking out what little light broke through the trees as the swarm of insects washed over them like a tide of small, writhing bodies.

Embedded in the tornado of flies, they flailed their limbs in wild panic as they tried to push onwards through the cloud of humming blackness and free themselves from harassment.

With lips clamped shut they dashed through the swarm, and insects crawled into nostrils and ears with a deafening buzz that sent their anxiety skyrocketing as they jerked and flinched at the disgusting assault.

Thrashing at the very air around them, Chris even igniting the blowtorch again to cut a swathe of flame ahead of them, they ran at full speed trying to break through the swarm that was moving along with them.

"Cut right," Rich shouted through the blackness as eager flies took this moment to fill his open mouth, crawling inside and buzzing across his tongue and throat.

Fighting back every urge to open his mouth, he sucked in his cheeks and drew all the saliva and bugs into a whirlpool at the back of his throat before releasing them with all the force he could muster into the air like a writhing spitball of pestilence.

Making the sharp detour on Rich's heels, they rushed forward and eventually broke free of the miasma of insects as the treeline became more sparce. Then they saw the rockface ahead of them, and with it, the entrance to the cave.

As with their first visit, the cave mouth was mostly blocked with large stones, leaving a person-sized hole to pass through.

Though this hole in the rock face was as unassuming as the last time, never had an entranceway evoked a more all-consuming level of dread.

Rich swallowed as they found themselves facing what felt like his own gateway to hell. The appearance of a tri-headed dog with a serpentine tail wouldn't entirely have surprised him.

"Abandon all hope, ye who enter here," Sophie croaked in a wizened voice as she stared into the mouth of the cave.

"Let's hope we don't have to actually pass through the nine circles of hell, though," Rich grimaced, still trying to shake the last of the flies from his body, "I'm not sure the ferryman will accept contactless."

"Well, it appears we can add swarms of insects and bringing fucking tree people to life to her list of abilities. I say we've earned another break before we step into whatever else she's got up her sleeves," Aaron said defiantly.

Sophie dropped to the dirt and began to inspect her wounded ankles, having barely had a moment to register the damage the thorny barbs of her earlier vine snare had left her with. Compared to how the guys were currently faring injury-wise, she didn't have a lot to complain about, but it was worth taking a look while they had the chance.

Aaron dropped down beside her with a grunt, his filth-encrusted smile still somehow carrying the boyish charm he affected so easily.

"how're you holding up, my little scum cookie?"

"I'm fine. Have you seen yourself?" Her well-maintained brows shot up as her eyes widened at him before she giggled in a manner that made Aaron's eyes widen, but clearly warmed him at the same time.

"I've definitely looked better; I'll give you that. Felt better too to be honest." He absently picked at a graze on his cheek as he looked down at her.

"You're gonna need a bathtub full of hand sanitizer to get yourself clean."

"Probably." His tongue probed his back teeth as he waited for her to stop fussing over her cuts. "Do you remember our first date?"

She gave him an odd look. "Are you asking me if I've gone senile? It wasn't that long ago, of course I remember. I haven't forgot about Dre either, in case you were curious." She smirked.

"When you dragged me along to go and get pierced."

"Yeah, I remember. I don't know what was funnier, your fear of getting a needle stuck through your ear, or your excitement at getting to see my tits on date one."

"The latter for me," he smiled. "And do you remember what you said?"

Her smile widened into a mischievous grin. "Yeah. Just the one nipple in case the date went well."

"Yeah. So what I'm thinking is, we started things out with a little pain and things went well from there. This is no different. We've had to endure some pain, but things are going to work out. We're coming back out of this cave."

Sophie's blank stare lasted a few seconds before she beamed a huge smile up at him. "You know, for the last couple of days you've ping-ponged between abject rage and juvenile humour, and now you're just gonna pull out stuff like that? Honestly, Aaron, and I mean this in the best possible way, you never cease to amaze me."

She brought herself up onto her knees and flung her arms around him before landing a huge kiss on his blood covered lips. "Sorry if this hurts."

Across from them, Dora stood staring back out into the forest behind her, part waiting for the insect swarm to find them, and part lost in her surroundings.

"We'd have missed the cave if we carried on running blindly through the woods in that cloud of bugs."

"Absolutely, we would." Rich placed a heavy hand on her shoulder as he moved to her side and gazed out across the woodland ahead of them. "It'd be nice to think she was trying to keep us away, but I'm not too sure she's exactly scared of this particular Scooby-Doo crew if I'm being honest."

"Jinkies." She chuckled, thankful for any moment of normality she could squeeze out of this hellish situation. "You know Velma was definitely a lesbian, right?"

"I never gave it much thought, really. I think I was more interested in one of those giant sandwiches that elongated your neck when you ate it." He patted his stomach playfully. "Maybe you and I can sneak off and find the kitchen in this cave while the others go and de-mask old man Withers?"

"Unlikely. Let's focus on getting in and out in one piece and I'll see what I can whip you up when we get home. A Scooby snack, if you will."

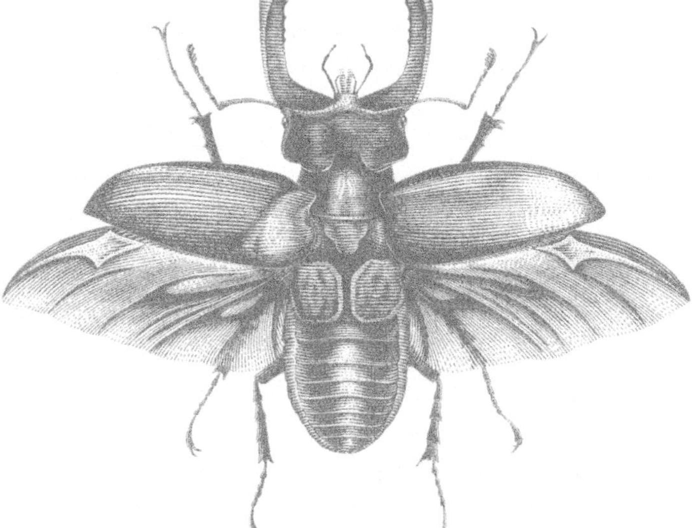

CHAPTER 28

A frigid wind blew from the mouth of the cave, washing over them as they stood ready to journey forward, weapons in hand and flashlights at the ready.

Behind them, a squirrel scurried up the trunk of a tree and came to a halt on a spindly branch ten feet from the ground as it curiously peered at the assembled group.

Bloody, beaten and bedraggled, the quintet was a far cry from the action heroes that would adorn any self-respecting movie poster. They were much closer to the wide-angle news helicopter footage of a group of hostages taking their first steps back into sunlight after their freedom from captivity.

Their faces were set with grim determination and the time had come to venture back into the cave and put an end to this ordeal one way or another.

"Shall we?" Aaron stepped out of line towards the hole, a white knuckled grip held firmly on the prehistoric spear that was hopefully their one trump card.

Dora skipped forward and spun, hands waving frantically. "Wait!"

"What is it?" Rich asked, his heartrate spiking for a moment.

"We need to be thinking smart with this. If she's going to come at us, we don't stand a chance in a confined space. I think it's best if Chris and I take front and rear, if we're as untouchable as it seems, then it stops us walking into danger."

"The very nature of what we're doing is walking into danger." Chris grimaced, his burnt and blistered face rebelling against the movement. "But I agree with you. I'll take the lead, at least I've been here before."

Aaron stepped to Chris with a sheepish look on his face and cleared his throat theatrically. "Chris, I actually do want to apologize. I know I've been a bit a tool to you, and I said some shitty stuff back at Victor's grandmas, but I'm glad I was wrong. You likely saved us again back there."

Chris flushed and stared at the ground, looking oddly ashamed. Rich frowned for a moment. Was Chris still feeling bad about the hotel goings-on?

"It's okay," Chris mumbled. "I did act like I was trying to save my own skin back there, so it's understandable. Let's all just try to make it out the other side of this."

With Chris now taking point, they stepped through one by one into the cave, the wind still whistling past them, carrying a fetid smell of death.

Inside the mouth of the cave, the breeze immediately halted as though it was never there, and the humid temperature inside was a jarring increase to the already warm weather.

The plant life that coated the ceiling and walls here was in misery, dry, yellowed and fighting for its life. An eerily similar mirror to the situation that they currently found themselves in.

Beyond tired of the constant threat of unknown attack, the group marched past the pendulous stalactites that coated the ceiling, readying flashlights as they moved further into the tunnel, losing the lingering light from the entranceway behind them.

With four flashlights between five of them, Aaron remained on the heels of Chris, the headlamp fastened around his head keeping his, and more importantly Chris's hands free to ready their weapons as he peered over Chris's shoulder to illuminate their passage of the tunnel as it tightened around them.

Before long the narrow tunnel walls became damp to the touch as the humidity began to spike and the very air around them became thick with the scent of mildew and decay. The same stagnant smell that permeated the kitchen where they'd found Francine's body.

As they marched on with only the sounds of their scuffling feet filling the tunnel around them, a low crackling sound like oil beginning to heat up in a pan began to emanate from all around.

Rich spun the beam of his flashlight to the wall on his left, illuminating the black vein-like patterning that was moving across the sides of the tunnel. Inky black tendrils were spreading like cancer along the wall, spiderwebbing as it continued, seemingly keeping pace with them as they moved.

"I think she knows we're coming." He turned around and shined the light in the direction they'd come from, half expecting some creeping demon to be closing on them from behind.

"I don't think the element of surprise was ever going to be on our side," Aaron called out over his shoulder.

"I don't think a lot of things have been on our side," Sophie muttered. Her eyes too were drawn to the spreading black nervous system of the cave growing alongside them.

Dora adjusted the torch that was affixed to her forehead and looked up at Rich, momentarily blinding him in the process. "Shit, sorry." She quickly angled it up towards the ceiling of the cave.

"Who have you got waiting for you, Rich?"

Rich blinked the spots out of his vision and gave her a puzzled look. "Come again?"

"Sorry, like when we get out of here. A girlfriend? Wife?"

"Oh." He paused for a second. "No, no girlfriend."

"Boyfriend? Apologies, no idea what your thing is." She gave him a weak smile, her gums peeking across the top of her teeth, and shrugged.

"No. it's ok." He sniffed as he thought about his response, inhaling a little too much of the stagnant air around him. "I don't really have a thing. Never have. I guess I'm just keeping myself alive for me."

"That's fair. Me too, I guess. Or maybe for spite."

Rich chuckled. "Spite works too, I suppose."

At the head of the party, Chris stopped abruptly, causing them to pile into each other unexpectedly.

He stroked the damp wall of the tunnel, his fingers passing through the soft moss and saturating his hand in droplets of cool water.

"We're not far from the pool now, I remember it getting damp and more moss-covered on the walls as we got close. Is everyone ready?"

Aaron squeezed past them to the front, having to awkwardly twist himself through in the still-confined tunnel. "As we'll ever be, but I'm going to take point from here. Let's be ready for some serious Meg Mucklebones shit, ok?"

"Thanks for that nightmare fuel," Sophie scoffed.

"Ahh, she's not as bad as that little ghost girl from Muppets Christmas Carol." He smirked.

"Okay, okay," Rich said as he pushed forward. "Can we leave the reminiscing about the fucked-up TV from our childhoods until we're done please."

"Atreyu drowning in The Neverending Story," Dora added, a wicked grin on her face.

Rich rolled his eyes. "Firstly, it was Artax. Atreyu was the kid; secondly can we just get going? I'd rather die out there than have to carry this on."

A sobering silence followed as it dawned on them that they might actually be marching to their deaths, but the reality of the situation also strengthened their resolve as they readied themselves to move forward again.

The brief moment of levity was sapped from them like a full exsanguination of joy as they began to tread forward slowly, lungs filled with held breath as each footstep crunched the earth below their feet.

Aaron stepped foot over foot like a stalking cat at the head of the procession as they turned the corner towards the very literal light at the end of the tunnel.

Above the sound of gravel scraping underfoot, a rhythmic drip, drip, drip of water began to fill the widening tunnel ahead of them moments before the delicate sound of singing carried into the tunnel.

Their blood ran cold as the soothing lullaby came to them, a soft mournful dirge echoing throughout the cave.

Off into the mountain cloud,
Where no rooster crows,
No dog shall bark, no cows bellow,
The storm she surely grows.

Weapons were gripped, white-knuckle tight, as Aaron turned back, the horror apparent on his face as he silently nodded to the group and commenced tiptoeing forward once more.

Moving along slowly behind, Rich could soon see into the cave ahead and the singing halted as he caught sight of its source.

In the middle of the damp, humid grotto was the woman they both sought and feared.

Poised gracefully like a fragile ballerina on pointed toes, she stood arms outstretched in welcome. Her long silken hair whipped around her as if in its own personal breeze and the long white dress clung to her body as though pinned by the same winds.

Her naked feet were barely touching the earth, the toes seemingly skimming the ground like she was floating. Her wide smile was a broad assault of pink gums and glowing white teeth as she beamed her sinister grin at them.

Aaron hesitantly dropped into the cave, axe and spear raised high, as the others followed suit behind, forming a line alongside as the woman's mouth became a brief, full lipped pout before she began to speak.

"In all my years, I've never had my prey return to me. So eager to see your demise, clearly, and who am I to deny you such an end?" Her cheeks rose as the bone-chilling leer began to stretch across her face once more, widening beyond human capability as the flesh began to split and tear.

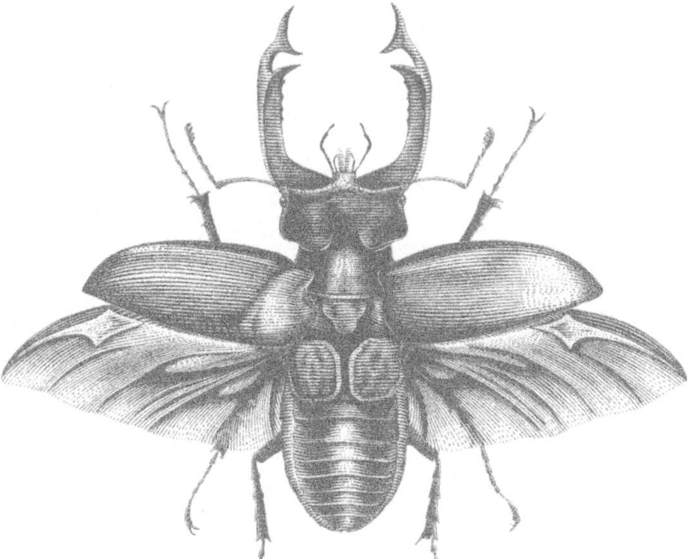

CHAPTER 29

A total lack of cohesive planning became abundantly clear as Aaron roared and charged forward, weapons at the ready.

The others followed suit, axes and hammers brandished as they ran, leaving only Chris behind, panic setting in as he fumbled with the dial on his handheld blowtorch.

The now gaping maw of torn flesh and jagged teeth spread wide as a guttural scream emitted forth from the woman's mouth.

An icy blast of air hit them as the gale force winds spewing from her lungs collided with the group and carried them off their feet, flying backwards and slamming them hard into the cave wall.

Feet still barely touching the ground, she moved forward, floating ominously towards them as her toenails left a long trail in the dirt beneath her.

Rich was first to shake off the impact and pulled himself up from the ground, casting a glace around as he watched the others slowly beginning to find their feet.

What was their plan?

They needed to try and break whatever that circle was around the hole. If this storm witch was being kept here like a prisoner or some medieval supernatural assassin, then their only hope was that in freeing her they would also free themselves in the process. They had no guarantees that it would work, but they were also out of other ideas, so it was their best shot.

The very present problem though, was the monstrous killing machine that they needed to get past first.

Seeing both Chris and Aaron back up on their feet, Rich took the lead and once again tried to rush the oncoming threat.

With unplanned military precision, the trio collided with the witch as she planted her feet and braced herself for the assault.

Rich brought the hammer down on the taloned hand that shot his way, as Aaron, to his left, arced the graphite axe towards her face.

Tilting her head back, she avoided the fall of the blade, her chin jutting to the sky as she flung out with her right hand at the same time, scraping pointed nails across Aaron's unguarded face.

Chris aimed a blast of fire towards the same arm, sending a conflagration of flames up her as the sleeve of her dress ignited.

Dora and Sophie, shaking off the impact from the blast, rushed into the fray, moving around behind her as they rained down blows on her back with their hammers.

Though the woman was of a slight frame, the hammer blows landed with a tough, spongey resistance and seemed to bounce back from each strike.

Whipping around in a circle, the witch spun her burning arm like a torch, forcing everyone back as she evaluated her attackers.

A heaving breath of ice-cold air spewed forth from her lips, dousing the flames on her arm as it hissed and smoked.

Taking advantage of their moment of hesitation she lunged forward, gripped Chris by the throat, and lifted him choking from the ground, arm still scorched and black from his attack.

An axe bit deep into the bicep of the muscular, grey arm holding him aloft as Aaron pressed the attack. Green-black sludge oozed from the wound, but completely unfazed, she turned her attention to him, her dark eyes narrowing as she gripped his wrist and twisted.

A sharp snapping of bone was followed by a tandem scream from both him and Sophie as Aaron fell to the ground clutching at his lifeless hand.

She stepped forward, Chris still dangling in the air, and after ignoring another hammer blow to the side from Rich she turned her attention to Dora, repeating the same lunge and again, lifting her from the ground by the throat.

"Let's see about you two, shall we?" she leered as she effortlessly cast them both into the pool. Waves splashed up around them as they hit the water and sunk beneath its stagnant surface.

Rich stiffened. His burst face would be vulnerable to a world of infection from that water, and even more importantly Chris' was no longer free from the witch's wrath.

A thought that was much more damning.

Seeming to forget everyone else for a moment, Sophie rushed to Aaron's side as he knelt, eyes fixed on his lifeless hand. Beads of sweat ran down his face as he gritted his teeth through the pain. His wrist radiated heat, the bones clearly snapped, but thankfully hadn't pierced the skin.

Rich swept up the fallen axe and sprinted to the woman, who was turning back from the pool, hate burning in the obsidian pinpricks of her soulless white eyes.

"Just fucking die, already!" He swung the axe and hammer, bringing them together like a pincer as the axe buried itself into her shoulder and the hammer collided with her face, snapping bone, and dislocating her jaw.

Her charred arm shot forward, a claw of sharp talons sinking into his shoulder and ripping at the flesh, blood running down her bony fingers as she withdrew the hand.

Rich reached for his arm and winced as he put pressure on the wound before he watched with disgust as the witch's jaw snapped back into place with a sickening pop as she raised the bloody hand to her mouth and lapped at the blood with a long, slimy tongue.

His stomach did somersaults as the sickness washed over him, but with gritted teeth he stepped up to his likely demise.

"Delicious," she rasped, Rich's blood now coating her lips.

"Yeah, I'm a veritable Christmas ham. Come get some," he shouted as he stepped forward, a wavering in his step as he tried to buy some time.

Chris flopped out of the pool, his now waterlogged clothes weighing heavily on him, and he looked to the exit tunnel from the cave.

Shame filled him at his natural cowardice. Not that it mattered now, he was truly part of this and there was no longer any place to run.

After turning back to the waters, he reached down and grabbed Dora under the arms as she thrashed wildly, panic setting in and pulled her from the pool.

Once out, he brought himself up onto his knees and gripped Dora by the shoulders, shaking her as she huffed short, staccato breaths through her nose, beginning to hyperventilate.

"Dora, you need to calm your breathing, take long slow breaths. We have to help them."

Chris looked up to see the witch stepping forward with precise, graceful steps as she closed the gap between her and Rich. Her normally slate coloured skin was cast in a yellow-green hue from the dim lighting in the cave and her hair whipped about violently around her.

"The most unlikely of heroes," she sneered, the alluring, dulcet tone of her voice carrying through the grotto. "Come forth in all your corpulent glory to protect your friends. How very noble. Noble and fruitless."

Yeah, maybe." Rich lunged forward, darting left at the last moment as he brought the axe around, cutting a wide sweep across her body and slicing the base of her neck as he stumbled to the ground.

Thick, black ichor poured from the gash at her throat as it opened up, running down her bony chest and soaking into the white gown before the wound sealed itself almost immediately.

Rich rolled with the fall, moving more gracefully than he probably ever had and landed on his back, gripping tightly onto both weapons.

Her hate filled eyes burned into his very soul like a looming figure of death as she leaned over his prone form as he swung out with both hammer and axe.

He missed with both and caught the brief flash of pale flesh and taloned fingers darting towards him before the pain erupted in his face.

He let out a blood-curdling scream as white-hot agony coursed through him and saw her once again standing tall as she held aloft a hand dripping with crimson blood.

His left eye dangled from a tendon-like red cord between her fingers before she dropped it into her waiting mouth and crunched it between her jagged teeth, a rivulet of pink jelly drooling down her lips.

A hammer slammed into the woman's side and harmlessly bounced off as she turned her attention to its sender – Sophie standing legs splayed, a look of bitter disgust on her face alongside Aaron who was slowly beginning to climb to his feet.

Licking her lips, the witch took a step towards them, and the full force of Chris slammed into her back, toppling her forward as she staggered, trying to maintain her balance.

While she span on the spot, a rush of wind coursed through the cave around her, she met Chris's terrified eyes as her hand shot forward and grabbed at his neck.

Her fist closed tightly over the soft flesh of his throat and she ripped it away, a horrifying tearing of sinew and muscle as the hand drew back with its prize.

A brief, bubbling gurgle emitted from Chris before a waterfall of thick, syrupy blood flooded from the gaping hole, dropping him to his knees before falling forward, face down in the dirt with a thud, dead before he hit the ground.

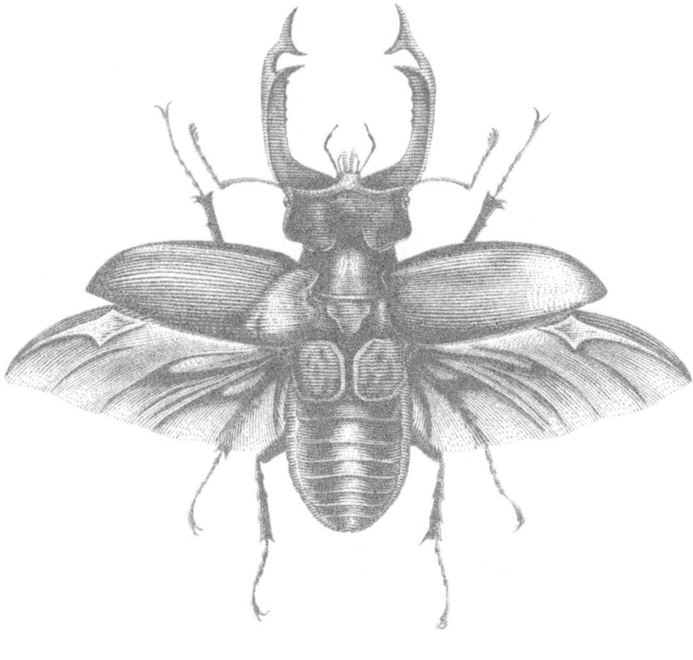

CHAPTER 30

A pool of blood spread across the stone cavern floor beneath Chris's lifeless body as time seemed to move in slow motion.

Screams from Sophie and Dora echoed off the walls of the cave, a deafening wail of anguish filling the chamber, both women brought to their knees as the dread and terror of the situation washed over them.

Clambering from the ground, thick blood seeping from his hollow eye socket, Rich brought himself up to a crouch, the burning pain in his shoulder pulsing rhythmically.

Aaron wavered on his feet, the fossilised dagger clenched hard in his left fist, his right arm hanging lifeless at his side.

Dora's banshee wail turned from anguish to rage as she focused her attention on the woman still grasping the pound of flesh in her fist. She ran forward, scooping up a fallen axe from the ground as she set her sights on the murderous witch before her.

"Get the fucking symbols!" Aaron bellowed, stepping towards the still-grinning woman as she nonchalantly cast aside the remnants of their friend.

Dora's axe carved into the back of the woman's thigh, providing a momentary distraction as Aaron lunged forward, dagger shard raised and sunk it through the witch's palm.

A high-pitched scream deafened him as the flesh burnt and hissed around the spear, smoke rising from the wound. The pungent stench of charred flesh and rot filled the cavern.

Rich stumbled and fell to ground, the skin on his palms grazing on the rough gravel. After forcing himself back to his feet, he headed towards the hole in the top of the cave as Sophie scrambled to pick up the hammer she'd thrown earlier.

A bony backhand sent Dora sprawling to the ground as the woman pulled her other hand free from the fossilised dagger and hit Aaron with a shrill scream as her jaw began to unhinge like a serpent.

Her throat bulged and pulsed as a wave of viscous sludge vomited forth from her mouth and slammed into Aaron with the force of a firehose.

Aaron was knocked to the ground, the blast of stagnant swamp water and writhing maggots coating him like some Lovecraftian afterbirth.

Rich tried to tune out the sound of his friends being tortured as he stared up at the hole above him. "Sophie, you need to get up on my shoulders."

She turned back to the sight of Aaron hitting the ground and froze, ready to change direction when she felt Rich's grasp on her arm.

"You can't help him. We've got to do this now while they're buying us time." Rich knew his pleading face was a blood-soaked nightmare.

"Shit. Okay, okay." She nodded as she turned to face Aaron, tears in her eyes as she parted her legs.

Rich ducked his head under her buttocks and brought all his weight up, lifting Sophie from the ground on his shoulders as he felt the wounds on his shoulder and stomach open as he tensed. Through gritted teeth he turned and manoeuvred them below the hole.

Dora once again dragged herself from the ground and charged forward with her axe, burying it deep into the back of the witch's ribs, where it sunk into spongy flesh before hitting bone.

Unbothered by the hit, the woman turned and grabbed a handful of Dora's hair in a tightly grasped fist before swinging her whole body at the nearest wall, where the wind was immediately knocked out of her as she slid down it.

Something inside her cracked as she hit the cave wall and pain resonated across her body as she landed face down in the dirt. Struggling to catch her breath she managed to bring herself up onto all fours as she heard footsteps heading her way.

A dark shadow fell across her before she was once again painfully lifted from the ground by her hair and flung towards the wall, slamming into it but managing to stay upright.

The woman closed the gap and pinned her by the throat to the wall, leaning in close and breathing stale breath into her face as she spoke. "I'm growing tired of this game, child. I think it's time you joined your beloved."

Dora raised her hands and began to wildly claw at the witch's arms, gouging into flesh with her nails as she wildly bucked and thrashed trying to break free from the chokehold that pinned her.

The air left her body as spindly fingers thrust into her flesh below her ribcage, the hand forcing itself inside her, worming upwards as pain wracked her body.

The coppery taste of blood filled her mouth as she choked, spitting blood into the witch's face as she coughed and spluttered, her eyes resolutely focused on the inky black pinprick pupils that stared back at her.

If she was going to die, then she would face it head on, fearless and unafraid.

Her pinned body shook and convulsed as she felt the intrusive hand inside her close into a tight grip.

A sharp pulling sensation was the last thing she felt before the life left her body and her head slumped forward.

Releasing the fistful of viscera in her grasp, the woman stepped back, letting Dora's lifeless body fall to the floor before turning to face Aaron, who was screaming bloody murder in her direction, a pool of writhing slime at his feet.

Coated entirely in bog-like scum and slime, a row of bleeding gashes running up the side of his face and his right arm hanging limply by his side, he raised the fossilised dagger in his left hand and grinned menacingly like a man possessed.

"If you're quite finished dealing with the people that can't defend themselves, why don't you come and try that with me?" he wobbled unsteadily on his feet, but the determination on his face showed no signs of fear. "Because I'm burying this thing so far down your throat that it's gonna burst out your putrid cunt."

A vicious smile split her face as she stepped forward, though it appeared to Aaron that her once tight and angular bone structure had dropped, the blue-grey skin sagging around the eyes and cheeks. Dark blood still dripped from the puncture wound in her hand as she raised both arms up, her nails elongating into sharp talons before his eyes.

Biting back the pain in his wrist, Aaron leapt forward ducking under the sweep of both arms and sank the dagger into her thigh, burying it deep into her flesh before pulling it out and jumping back to avoid her reach.

Green slime bubbled from the wound as smoke rose from the hole, sizzling like fat in a pan as gore oozed down her thigh.

An anguished howl of pain erupted from her lips as Aaron watched her skin continue to slip, deep bags appearing under her eyes and the flesh around her mouth becoming jowly. The stony tint of her flesh looked to be weakening into a sickly, jaundiced yellow.

Having seen and felt the immense strength she possessed, he knew he had to stay out of reach of her iron grasp. A single twist from her strong hands could easily shatter bone.

Lunging forward again, he swiped out with the dagger at her arm, missing at the last moment and catching a clawed hand across the face, grazing his cheek, and painfully slicing the side of his nose, splitting his nostril.

In a flurry of hit and run attacks they traded blow for blow, neither one managing more than cuts and scrapes on the other as they danced around the cave.

The immediate effects of blood loss were taking a much stronger toll on Aaron, and the wooziness he was feeling was going to catch up to him eventually.

He just needed to buy a little more time.

Mustering all the strength he could manage, he charged forward, head low into a full tackle, bringing the spike up to drive it into her chest, ignoring her arms closing around him.

The tip of the fossil pierced her chest moments before she shifted, tilting away from the strike, her left arm grasping at Aarons broken wrist and squeezing as the already broken bones shattered further.

Dragging him by the lifeless arm, she brought her right hand upwards in a taloned cleave that ripped across Aarons body, carving deep incisions into his chest tearing both fabric and flesh before rocking him backwards towards the ground.

Rich wobbled and weaved as Sophie reached up to the ceiling and swung the graphite hammer at the symbols carved into it.

"Fuck's sake," she shouted as the hammer again hit nothing but air. Beads of sweat ran down her face as she tried to raise herself up, unsteadily on Rich's shoulders.

The sound of Aaron's enraged screams filled the cave behind them, and they both felt the panic of time running out.

Another swing grazed the stone carving of a bird in combat with a snake, and as the hammer failed to land, Rich was lurched forward by the momentum of Sophie's swing.

"Fuck, I nearly had it. Are you okay, Rich?"

"Don't worry about me, just get it done. Hurry!" He could feel the wet trickle of blood running down his shoulder and stomach, the burning ache of his injuries a constant reminder of his fragility, and it felt like all the remaining blood currently resided in his face. His cheeks were flushed, and pain pulsing in his temples.

The next blow once again remained on target but fell frustratingly short of the stone. Her aim was fine, but it was just out of reach. "It's no good, I can't reach it."

Rich craned his neck up and looked at the gaping hole above him as he reached to cup the underside of Sophie's feet. "Get ready. You get once chance at this," he puffed as he braced himself, pain burning in his cuts as he tensed.

"3."

"2."

"1."

Dropping his neck forward, he pushed with all his might as he raised his arms, catapulting Sophie skyward.

Suddenly propelled upwards, shaking as she lost the stability of Rich below her, she flew through the air, hammer swinging in flight like a gothic Thor.

The flat of the hammer caught the edge of the opening where the symbol was carved, and shattered the stone, breaking the intricate design away from the rock and bringing one of the inlaid gemstones with it as Sophie careened towards the ground, arms flailing.

She ate dirt as she landed, face rocking into the solid cave floor and splitting her cheek on the hard stone beneath.

Rich rushed to her aid as an unnatural blast of cold air rushed into the hole and almost took him off his feet, the wind whipping through him like a tornado as it funnelled into the cave.

With a bright flash of light from above and sudden rolling thunder, the heavens opened as rain hammered down through the hole, whipping erratically in the wild flourish of wind.

A real storm was about to begin.

Rich helped her up from the dirt, and they turned to face their adversary.

What had Victor's grandmother called her? *vrajitoare furtuna.*

Storm witch.

The woman stood in the centre of the cave, brow furrowed, midnight black pupils staring through them.

Raised up tall, arms outcast as the blast of wind hit her, she appeared to have grown in stature – her already imposing height now a statuesque nightmare.

Once grey skin was now a vibrant, ice blue and the tight, angular bone structure had returned, dark grooves highlighting the muscle across her shoulders and arms as she grinned a wide, sinister smile of now perfect white teeth, the pink of her tongue and gums popping against the darkness of her skin.

Equal parts ethereal being and demonic entity, she basked in the rain and wind that whipped around her.

"Freedom," she bellowed. "No longer bound and abused like a lowly serf. Never again to serve as a thrall to weak willed puny mortals." The air around her crackled with static as tiny lightning storms danced within the fierce gale that encircled her god-like form. "This land with know my reckoning and it will fear me."

She punctuated the four final words with slow, deliberate venom as the watching pair felt the cold chill of dread run down their spines.

Frozen in terror and helpless to do anything but watch, they remained under the hole, the pounding rainfall assaulting them as they waited for death.

Rich waited for his life to flash before his remaining eye, but nothing came. No recap of a life squandered and wasted.

Sophie thought of Aaron, the sarcastic, goofy idiot that she'd loved, and the caring soft side that only she saw. She didn't believe in an afterlife, but if she was going to die, then at least they would be reunited in that.

The woman levelled her gaze at the pair, who were both stricken with terror as they watched her reinvigoration, lowering her arms before taking a step forward, the full might of her power once again flowing through her veins.

It was time to clean up the loose ends before unleashing true revenge onto a world that had known complacency for too long.

Like lambs to the slaughter, their eyes widened in horror as she stepped patiently forward, the rhythmic clicking of her long nails sounding a consistent taunt.

She would savour these two.

A twisted, joyful glee warmed her as she considered all the tortures she would soon inflict, when a sudden impact rocked her forward.

CHAPTER 31

Aaron pounced, his mangled wrist dangling as he threw the arm around the witch's shoulder, pulling tightly into her throat with his forearm as he swung the left arm around her other side, the fossilised dagger gripped in his fist as he sank it deep into her chest.

A banshee's wail shook the whole cavern as she threw her head back and screamed, the storm still raging out of control around her.

With every fading ounce of energy he had left in his body, Aaron clung on for dear life as she thrashed and convulsed against him, spitting hate and fury as she tried to shake him free.

His left hand trembled and shook as he continued to force it into her chest, agony flaring across his body as he pulled too with his useless right arm, driving the jagged point towards the witch's heart with the weight of his entire body.

Rich and Sophie watched as Aaron hung from the witch's back, her cries and screams yielding no results. She seemed to deflate as she thrashed, the once Amazonian stature melting away as he buried the spike into her body.

Her flesh washed out to a sickly yellow as it began to loosen and sag about her face, transforming the hauntingly beautiful women into a decrepit crone. Her once flowing ashen locks dulled and flopped becoming lank strings of greasy dark hair plastered to her face and her wrinkled and cracked lips encircled a mouth of crooked brown teeth.

Thick green Ichor oozed from the hole in her chest and poured from her nose and mouth, her screams reduced to a series of gurgling moans as the strength ebbed from her body.

Aaron hung on, feeling the fight go out of her as she slowly sunk lower and lower as he continued to pull the spike back towards his body, managing to bring both arms together in a crushing bearhug, driving it into her heart.

The nauseating stench of rot and decay flooded the cavern as her wretched fluids washed down over his arms, her wails now little more than a whimper.

Reduced to his knees, he felt the tip of the spear reach through her body and graze his chest as he closed the grapple tighter before she burst, rupturing into a tidal wave of stagnant gore that washed over him as he collapsed backwards onto the dirt.

Mesmerised and disgusted by the display before them, Rich and Sophie watched the woman explode into a shower of sludge as Aaron fell backwards.

Forcing back the urge to vomit, they staggered across the cave towards Aarons lifeless body.

Splayed out like a discarded ragdoll and coated in an ocean's worth of pond scum, Aaron looked battered and broken. His blood-soaked face was a series of deep cuts and scrapes, and his t-shirt was shredded to reveal deep gashes across his chest.

It didn't look like he was breathing.

Sophie dropped to her knees and began to vigorously shake him by the shoulders. "Aaron, babe, come on, you did it. Don't you fucking die on us."

Rich glanced about the cave, the foul stench of death still heavy in the air.

Chris's body, throat completely shredded and torn, lay face down in the dirt, and Dora was slumped against the wall she had slid down. Her lifeless eyes stared out into oblivion, and Rich felt a stabbing in his chest that completely broke him, his good eye welling up with tears.

"Aaron come on, please, don't try and pull some martyr shit on me." Sophie pounded on his chest as she wept.

With a gasping inhale of breath, he bolted upright. "Ghhhhhhh... you miss one hundred percent of the shots you don't take," he blurted before falling back down, eyes remaining focused on Sophie.

"What the fuck, Aaron? You let me think you're dead and then come out with that?" Her expression of anger was one he knew to be entirely for show, and Aaron could see the relief in her face.

He coughed and gave her a wavering smile. "You know I'd die for you."

"Don't you dare," she scolded. "that's not happening. It's just a thing people say, like we'll stop if it hurts."

Aaron's nose wrinkled, causing a pulse of blood from his damaged nostril. "It smells like bigfoot fucked a skunk in an unplugged fridge around here."

"There he is." Rich laughed, coming to stand over the injured pair.

"Did we win?" Aaron asked, scrunching his eyes tightly as another wave of pain hit him.

Rich knelt next to Sophie and reached under Aaron's bad arm to help lift him carefully from the ground, gently easing him up as he groaned in pain. "I guess you could call it that." His voice broke. "I just wish the toll wasn't so high."

The pair heaved him from the stone floor, and with an arm over each shoulder readied themselves for the long and painful trek back to civilisation.

They would have to come back for Dora, Chris, and Jack. The trio deserved a hero's funeral, but at the very least they could have the dignity in death that they had earned.

Grace and Francine, too, would need to be taken care of.

Rich's head started to swim at the notion of trying to explain all this and he tried to banish those thoughts to the dark recesses of his mind.

That was a future problem.

Right now, they just needed to get the sorely required medical attention and worry about the details and explaining later.

They hadn't done anything wrong, and five of their friends had been needlessly killed.

To hell with the red tape.

It was going to be a slow and agonising journey, but the weight of dread was now lifted from their shoulders.

"What do you say we get you to a hospital, buddy?" Rich asked as he noticed Aaron taking a long, hard look at his decimated eye socket.

"Aye, aye, captain." Aaron smirked.

"Oh, fuck you, Aaron." Rich chuckled, as the blood soaked and beaten trio began to hobble towards the tunnel and their long walk to freedom.

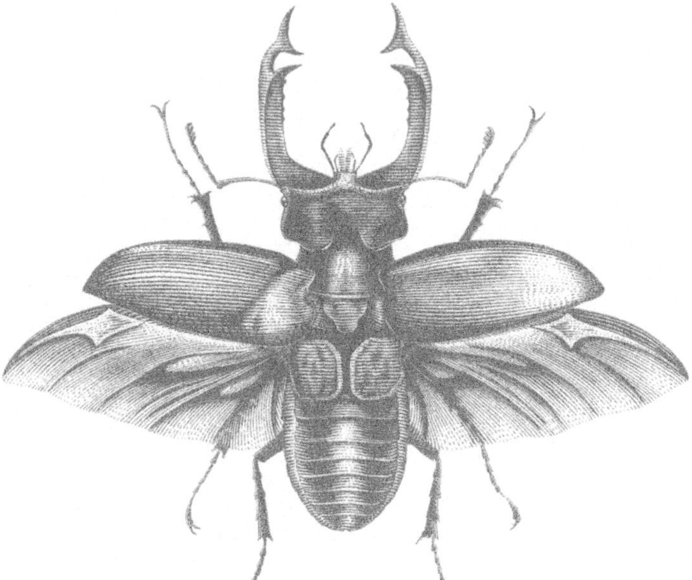

ACKNOWLEDGMENTS

Here's the thing with acknowledgements – You will invariably forget someone.

From a telescopic standpoint, I would like to thank John Carpenter, Wes Craven, David Cronenberg, George Romero, and David Lynch for their service to horror on screen; you're just a handful from the many who helped grow my love of horror movies. For their services to horror in the form of the printed word, I would have to include Clive Barker, Stephen King, James Herbert, and Joe Hill as standout authors, but none come close to Robert McCammon, who has captivated my love of horror fiction for as long as I can remember.

Up close and personal (so close you can feel me breathing down your neck) I would like to thank Jess for once again turning my flurry of words into a serviceable book, Chris and Brady for the incredible cover art and lush interior of this chunk of dead tree you have just read, and Ben for proofreading away my mistakes like a literary hitman. I couldn't have asked for a better A-Team.

Finally, to you, for reading this book. If you're a horror enthusiast, I hope I did it justice. If you're not, I hope it provided you with a little terror for your day.

About the Author

A.D Jones lives in the North of England; where he spends his time favoring books over people and can be found writing or devouring said books to review online. He loves Coca-Cola, Twin Peaks, all things horror, and cult movies. He dislikes the movie *'The Karate Kid'* with a passion that burns brighter than the sun.

His debut novel – **Umbrate** was released in 2023 and can be found on Amazon.

You can find him on Instagram - The_Evergrowing_Library

REVIEWS

Reviews are the lifeblood of authors, and if you enjoyed this book and feel like championing the cause, then please consider leaving a review on Goodreads, Amazon, or any of your social media accounts. The book community is a magical place and it's truly a joy to read your thoughts.

Printed in Great Britain
by Amazon